Throughout Spanish California, when military tyrants sought to gain plunder from peaceful settlers, there emerged one man who gave them courage to fight oppression! That man was Zorro, a masked rogue who kept the people's enemies at bay with a flashing sword and a dashing smile.

Some people called him a 'bandit.' But others insisted the only things Zorro ever stole were the hearts of admiring *señoritas* — and of one tavern-owner in particular.

He carved the symbol of a 'Z' to mark the oppressors and scoundrels, but he left an indelible mark among the female populace. Though he may have saved their lives, women always found a certain emptiness in the remainder of their days when he rode away into the night.

Becoming ZORRO®

Susan Kite

Perego
Cover and Illustrations

Bill Cotter
Foreword

Audrey Parente
Editor

Zorro created by
Johnston McCulley

Bold Venture Press

Perego
Cover and story
illustrations

Audrey Parente
Editor

ISBN: 978-1-966085-24-9 (trade paperback)
ISBN: 978-1-966085-25-6 (case hardcover)

Available in eBook, paperback, case laminate hardcover, and dust jacket hardcover

Published by Bold Venture Press
www.boldventurepress.com

CONTENTS

Becoming Zorro: Could You? ... *Foreword by Bill Cotter* 9

Lessons In Honor .... *Introduction by Susan Kite* 15

Return With Honor .... *Susan Kite* 17

The European Method .... *Introduction by Susan Kite* 45

European Encounter .... *Susan Kite* 47

California Encounter .... *Susant Kite* 81

About the author: Susan Kite 141

About the author: Bill Cotter, introduction 142

About the illustrator: Perego 144

This one's for Guy Williams,
who brandished the sword
with a smile.

"BECOMING ZORRO" – COULD YOU ?

Foreword by Bill Cotter

The moment I heard the title of this book I was intrigued. *Becoming Zorro*. Wow. I likely had dreamed of being the swashbuckling hero when I first saw the Guy Williams show in my childhood years. I probably just thought all I would have to do is put on a cape and mask, but over the years I have often thought about how hard that would actually be.

I have seen most of the Zorro films and television series, including the early silent films, the Republic serials, and the modern epics. My favorite, though by far, is the Disney version, so I was excited to see author Susan Kite use that as the setting for this tale.

In 1976, I had the pleasure of wandering through the *Zorro* sets, which were still standing on Disney's backlot in Burbank. Disney had flown me out from New York for a job interview, and when a gap opened up between meetings they told me to pass the time walking around the lot. When I turned a corner and saw the *cuartel* set standing there, I just couldn't believe it. There are no words to describe how I felt walking through the very gates my hero had entered time and time again. I'm glad I didn't get too wrapped up in things and miss my next appointment, because Disney hired me. In August of that year, I was living in Burbank and visiting the set quite often.

Over the years I had the pleasure of meeting many of the cast and crew who had brought the shows to life. At times we would sit on the *cuartel* steps and talk about how the show came to be and some of the challenges they faced in filming it. One subject I can't recall discussing, though, is how Don Diego became Zorro. It was there in the story and it was filmed — pretty simple, or so it seemed. But let's think, just for a moment, about how it would be you or I — or pretty much anyone we know — set out to become Zorro.

First of all, as the book you are holding begins, you must have a burning desire to do so. It's a reasonable conclusion that people just don't wake up one day and decide to put on a cape and ride out to fight evil. There has to be a pretty strong reason. In the Disney series we saw how Diego came to his decision pretty quickly, all because of a letter from his father about unjust conditions back home. For me it would have taken a bit more than that, but such are the limitations of a 30-minute show. Even if you had years of watching and studying a problem like Monastario, though, could you easily become Zorro?

No matter how highly motivated you were, you would need to possess some pretty incredible athletic skills. That would pretty much rule me out right there. My proven lack of talent in things like baseball and lacrosse would indicate that my skills with a sword would likely be just as unsuccessful. Who knows, though? I might have a hidden gene that made me great with a sword. I don't expect to ever find out, as the only time I can recall ever holding a sword was examining one of Zorro's in the Disney Archives. And yes, in case you are wondering — I did make a "Z" in the air.

So, assuming you have the motivation and the skills, what is the next hurdle? Well, you must make sure you are independently wealthy and don't need to work at a real job. Your boss likely wouldn't be happy and would surely notice if you kept going to them to ask for time off for something you couldn't explain. "Excuse me, I need to run out right now, yet again, but I can't tell you why or when I'll be back." Yes, being wealthy and not working is an absolute must. Batman could never afford all the bat gadgets if not for Bruce Wayne's very convenient riches. If you, by any chance, are so wealthy that you can afford to become a caped hero, please do let me know. I might want to be your aide.

Which, of course, brings us to Bernardo, or in Batman's case, Robin. You absolutely need a stalwart companion who will not hesitate to risk

Bill Cotter holds one of the Walt Disney Company's many awards.

their life in the pursuit of your enemies. That friend also needs superior athletic skills and not have a traditional job. Just running through my list of friends I can't think of anyone ready or able to sign up.

Let's assume you get all of these things sorted out. What's next? Well, you better be single and planning on staying that way. Just like asking for time off from work, breaking dates to ride off into the night, no matter how valiantly, is likely to end most romantic entanglements. That is, unless, you are prepared to break a cardinal rule of being a caped hero and you reveal your great secret. The romance blossoms and a happy marriage follows. You are all set, right?

Wrong! Your newly acquired Significant Other is likely to start resenting your running out in the middle of dinner; when you have tickets to a show; when you promised to finally do some chore around the house, etc. I get called out as a first-responder and my wife has had to put too many meals into the refrigerator, or she attended events without me — and she doesn't have to worry about an army of lancers chasing after me as my mighty horse and I leap across a canyon.

Well, perhaps that obstacle can be overcome. That's fine until kids come along. "Sorry, son, I would like to play a game of catch but daddy has to go rescue someone from banditos." Telling your kids that would not be a good idea, for besides making them resent you, they are likely to get into an argument and say something like "My dad can beat up your dad because my dad is Zorro!" Or you could just not tell him why you ride off and leave him alone, but then it might be hard to explain all the cuts and bruises after your battles.

Nope. Becoming Zorro is not for me. There are simply way too many challenges and way too many risks. Luckily for the people of the Pueblo de Los Angeles, though, Don Diego de la Vega was a better man than I am. Turn the page and enjoy seeing how Zorro's story began.

BECOMING
ZORRO

LESSONS IN HONOR

Introduction by Susan Kite

Zorro, (Spanish for fox), sprang from the fertile imagination of author Johnston McCulley. In the first published story, the masked vigilante was already grown and enforcing his justice on criminals and corrupt officials in the pueblo de Los Angeles in the early 1800's.

McCulley's story, *The Curse of Capistrano* was spread out over five issues of *All-Story Weekly* in 1919. Here Don Diego Vega became disgusted with the way the crooked leaders of the community took unfair advantage of its citizens, donned a mask and an all-black disguise. Since that time, there have been numerous films, serials, books, magazines, cartoons, and TV programs celebrating justice and fairness by the masked defender, Zorro. The stories in this book are based on the characters and stories in the 1957-59 television series presented by Walt Disney.

Whichever version is used, the question is the same ... Where did this quest for inner justice come from? Where did a rich man's son learn his sense of honor and fair play? Did something happen that would later cause him to jump to the aid of the downtrodden?

That is the premise of *Return with Honor*, the beginning for young Diego who becomes a hero when he learns self-control and discipline at the tender age of ten.

RETURN WITH
HONOR

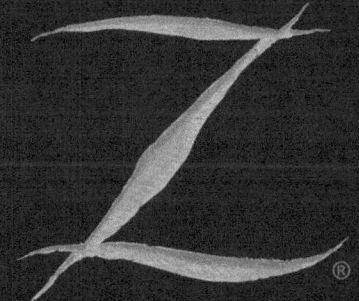

1

At San Pedro harbor, Diego de la Vega stood next to his father and watched the sun rising over the California hills. The light seemed to tinge the brush a fiery red. The younger man watched avidly, trying to remember every color, every shade, along with the smells and sounds of his homeland. The harsh calls of seagulls and jays sounded as though they were trying to outdo each other as they searched among the docks for their breakfast.

"Son, we won't see each other for over four years. It will feel like an eternity for me, but shorter for you. Make the best of that time. Learn everything you can to make this land even greater than it already is. Diego, my son, return with honor…" Alejandro stopped suddenly, as though he couldn't say more.

Diego gazed into his father's face and then back up toward the distant hawk. Yes, he remembered the time when honor became more than just a word. The time not too long before Mother's death….

Diego wiped his sleeve across his face and looked up. Manuel, Don Sebastian's oldest son, was standing over him, hands on his hips, a look of triumph on his face. "You wallow like some *peon's* pig, Diego de la Vega. Who taught you to fight? Rosarita?" the larger boy sneered. Then he threw back his head and laughed uproariously.

A fiery rage consumed Diego's heart and forced hot tears of defeat to the corners of his eyes. Blinking fiercely, he raised his sleeve to wipe the offending moisture away and saw the blood on his sleeve.

"Go home, *niña*. Go home to your mama. Let her read her precious books to you and sing to you. Leave the fighting to men," Manuel taunted. Turning to the little *peon* boy cringing in the dust, he commanded, "Go, and next time I tell you to do something, you will do it. Do you understand?" The *peon* nodded, his eyes wide with fear. He scuttled backwards on his bottom for a few feet, his eyes never leaving Manuel's face, before finally jumping to his feet and running down the dusty road.

"Go, Diego. Let us see how much dust you can kick up," Manuel said, turning his attention back to his opponent.

"That was a cruel trick, Manuel, putting those stones in your fists," Rosarita said hotly. She stood waving her finger in front of the larger boy's face.

Manuel grabbed her outstretched hand and jerked her close to him. "I will not be told what to do by either a weak mother's boy or a girl. Do you understand me?"

Rage forced Diego into action. His red-hot fury unabated, he jumped to his feet and drove his fist toward the larger boy's stomach. It never reached its destination. Manuel shoved Rosarita aside and grabbed Diego's fist, his fingers becoming like the steel jaws of a trap, clamping down on the younger boy's hand, squeezing Diego's fingers until the knuckles popped and he grunted with pain.

"You want to fight some more, *chica*? That is no problem to me," the bully sneered, squeezing harder.

Diego gasped at the fierce pain that radiated up his wrist and arm, but he clamped his lips together and refused to make an utterance. He drew back his left hand and slammed it against Manuel's cheek. With a roar of rage, the older boy released Diego for a moment and then grabbed him by the collar and shook him. Diego felt his teeth rattle. Manuel threw him to the dusty ground and began kicking him. Over and over again, without respite, the leather boots imprinting his soul with shame.

Rosarita grabbed the bully's arms, but she was thrown aside as easily as the wind scatters thistle down. Diego could only cover his head with his arms and take the punishment. The individual pains merged into one large one. The indignation of only moments ago turned into fear. *Is Manuel going to kill me?*

"Stop that!" a voice cried out. Diego barely heard it, only understanding that the terrible punishment was finally over. His breath came in choking gasps.

"He started it!" Manuel cried.

"Whether he did or not, I am stopping it. Go home, Manuel. I will talk to your father later."

Vaguely Diego heard the thudding of boot steps going down the road.

"Diego! Diego!"

His head pounding, Diego was unaware of who was calling his name. *A priest? Oh, Madre de Dios! Am I dying that I need a priest?* He felt gentle hands picking him up. He moaned and then clamped his torn lips together, refusing to give voice to his pain. To give his tormentor any more cause against him. He was being cradled against soft cloth, a warm body. "Father?" he asked softly, not opening his eyes.

"No, Diego, it is *Padre* Immanuel. I am taking you to the rectory to examine you, my son. Just relax, everything will be all right." Diego finally cracked open his eyes, finding the task infinitely difficult, and studied the kindly face of one of Los Angeles' resident priests. The cleric's sandy-colored hair shone like a halo and his smile reassured the beaten boy. Diego relaxed in the man's strong arms.

"Diego was just trying to help a *peon*. Manuel was beating the boy because he dropped his bridle," Rosarita explained, pattering alongside the priest.

"It is a good thing to have a noble heart, my son, but it is impossible even for a bravehearted hare to fight a lion in open combat," Father Immanuel said gently as he entered his room. Carefully he laid Diego on his pallet and directed Rosarita to light several candles. The priest pulled back the cloth coverings of his window, letting the light stream into the room. Opening a small wardrobe, he pulled out a leather bag and set it next to the battered boy.

Turning to Rosarita, he told her, "You go on home, *señorita*. If you see Don Alejandro, let him know where his son is." Rosarita stared at Diego. "*Señorita*, this young *caballero* will yet live to defend the honor of *peons* and young ladies," he added, smiling reassuringly at the girl.

She smiled back at the priest, then nodded to Diego and left.

"Diego, does anything feel like it's broken?" Father Immanuel asked.

Diego shook his head, but then stopped. There was a pain in his head that matched places on his body. "I don't think so, *Padre.*"

"Well, let me check and see, my boy." Carefully, the priest manipulated and prodded various places on his body. Diego winced when Father Immanuel felt the fingers on his right hand. "I feel no breaks, but I believe that young Manuel Gavilan may have strained the joints of this hand. You will need to be careful for a few days." A short while later, the priest sat back and perused the boy. "I believe you will live, young de la Vega, but you will be sporting a few bruises for a while."

Diego sat up, feeling stiff and sore in every part of his ten-year-old body. "*Gracias, Padre.*"

"Diego, the wind cannot bring down the juniper by blowing directly against it. The wind defeats the juniper by blowing the earth away from its roots. You cannot hope to defeat the likes of Manuel Gavilan by trying to fight against his brute strength." As Diego left the church, he wondered what he meant by the wind and the juniper tree.

***

"Do you understand what to do, Pedro?" Diego asked. Pedro nodded. Diego looked up and saw large grins on the faces of the other boys as they huddled together. There were six of them, all about the same age; boys from *hacendado's* houses and from the *vaqueros'* quarters, all Diego's friends. All of them sported wolfish grins of anticipation, deciding strategy in the stable yard of the de la Vega *hacienda.*

"Lupe and Juan will grab Manuel's legs, Pedro and Jose well grab his arms, Jorge, you will grab him around the waist. You have the longest arms," Diego instructed. His eyes glowed. Finally, he was going to get the revenge he so strongly desired. That was all he had thought about for the two weeks it had taken him to fully recover from Manuel's beating.

"And you will give Manuel the same that he gave you," Jorge said with a laugh. He went into a fighter's stance and struck an imaginary foe with his fists. "First with the right hand. *Pow!* Right in the stomach. Then with the left hand, right under the jaw. Over and over again. Let him feel what it is like to be beaten."

"Let *who* feel what it is like to be beaten?" a low voice asked.

Turning in alarm, Diego saw his father approaching from the outside gate. "Uh, hello, Father."

"Manuel, Don Alejandro," Lupe, the youngest, piped up.

"Oh?" Alejandro raised his eyebrows in interest. His once dark brown hair was shot with gray, but his walk was still vigorous as he drew near the boys. "I think your scheming is over for the day. You boys go home. Carlos will accompany you two," Alejandro said, looking at Lupe and Jorge, sons of local *hacendados*. The rest of you, go see if your parents have something for you to do." The boys scattered until only Diego and his father stood in the open area of the stable.

"My son, what is this you were planning?"

Diego looked toward the ground. "We were going to get Manuel back for beating me up," he said quietly. Somehow, Diego knew Father wouldn't like his plans very much.

"Did Manuel beat up just you, or did he beat up all six of you at one time?" Alejandro asked. Diego realized his father had heard all of their plans.

"Just me, but Father…"

"Diego, what honor is there in six of you ambushing and beating one, even if that one is a bully?"

"Father, I cannot defeat Manuel by myself. He is too big and strong."

"Diego, that is not the point. How would such a victory feel?"

Sighing, Diego looked up at his father. "I suppose I would still feel I had not defeated him myself," he said. "But Father, how can I beat him? He is not much older than I, but he is so much bigger and stronger."

"My son, it is my thought that you have been devoting so much time to studies that you have neglected to build your physical strength." Alejandro stroked his beard.

"But Father, you have said how important education is to the running of a rancho." Diego protested, but felt elation growing. *To be as strong as Manuel. Then I can beat him to a pulp!*

"*Sí*, it is, my son, but you must also have the physical strength to run a *rancho* as well. You must have the stamina to ride all day after the cattle and horses. You must be strong enough to hold the steers when you have roped them. You must have strength to hold on to this beautiful land that God has granted us. Do you understand, Diego?"

"*Sí*, Father."

"Perhaps you need to work at building your strength, and then when the time comes, you will be able to defend yourself against the likes of Manuel Gavilan. But son, always remember to fight your battles honorably."

"But Manuel does not fight honorably," Diego protested. "He hid rocks in his fists."

"You are correct, Diego, he does not. Some will always prey on the weak. That is why it is up to those of us who have more power to help those who are less fortunate."

"That's what I tried to do, Father."

CHAPTER TWO

"I know, Diego." He put his arm around his son's shoulders. This son of his, who looked so much like his wife, Isabella, who had so much of her intelligence, and her spirit, warmed his heart. He felt the heart of a lion beating in the small body close to his side. "Diego, I was very proud of the way you stood up for the *peon* boy's rights. That, too, is the sign of a good leader. But it does no good to try to stand up for someone's rights; you must be able to succeed.

"Right now, you are letting Manuel determine where and when you fight. You let him goad you into a fighting rage and then you are ready to be beaten. To defeat him, you must be the one to determine the battle," Alejandro admonished.

"How will I do that, Father? Will that happen when my body is stronger, when I can fight better?"

"No. If you think before you act and if you let your heart help you decide, you will know the time. Do not seek a fight, but when the time is right, and if the cause is honorable, do not run away from it."

***

"Diego, shall we read some more of the story of *El Cid*?" Isabella de la Vega asked. She watched her son fingering the hilt of one of Alejandro's swords. Although he had not yet been taught to fence, she could see in his small frame a natural grace that would make him a very good swordsman someday. Her only son was growing up so fast. She watched him touch the place on his cheek that had only recently turned back to its natural color. The green and purple bruises had been a continual embarrassment to him long after his cut lip and sore hands and muscles had healed. "Diego."

As he turned, Isabella saw a look of deep shame in his eyes. "Diego, come here, please," she said. Still holding the sword, he walked across the library and stood in front of her. "Diego, you are still thinking about Manuel Gavilan?"

"*Sí*, Mother. Father says that if I become stronger, I can defeat Manuel," Diego declared. "But I do not think I can ever become that strong," he added with a sigh.

"Maybe not, my son," she said, remembering her conversation with her husband just the previous night. She was chagrined Diego had apparently only remembered a small part of Alejandro's admonitions. In her heart, she hoped her son would remember more than revenge as he began his quest to be stronger. She saw so much more for her son than proving himself to the neighboring bully. She saw a compassionate heart, a will to do right, to be a leader. Her heart swelled. There was so much of Alejandro's fire, passion and spirit in this son of theirs. She was so proud of him. Tears of pride and joy stung her eyes, and she turned away to dab them with her handkerchief. "Diego, have you ever watched a fox hunt?"

"Sí, Mother. I saw one in the hills last winter."

"Describe it to me."

Diego paused a moment to think of what he had seen. "He was still, moving his head to hear. His eyes were on a place far ahead. The fox moved quietly, one step at a time. Very slowly. Then he was like lightning, running so fast he was almost a blur. He leaped into the air, pouncing on the grass. And suddenly he had a rabbit in his mouth."

There was a silence for a few moments as Diego gazed at her, waiting for her to comment. Isabella turned back to her painting. "And when something is chasing the fox?"

"Father said he saw a coyote chasing a fox one time."

"What did he say happened? After all, a coyote is larger and likely just as quick."

"He said the fox ran among the rocks, over a shallow river, through a field, but the coyote continued after him, not far behind."

"So, you're saying the coyote won?"

"No, Father said the coyote didn't win. He didn't catch the fox."

"How did the smaller fox get away?"

"Father said he climbed a tree. The coyote couldn't follow. Finally, the coyote left."

"Wonderful, the fox won!" Isabella gazed into her son's eyes. "Why do you think he won, my son? He is smaller, you know. The coyote has bigger teeth."

Diego gazed at the polished wooden floor. "First, he kept moving around, not letting the coyote catch him."

"But that didn't work."

Diego's eyes lit up. "He used his talent of climbing trees to get away."

"Yes, he used his talents. Was there anything else that helped the fox's escape?"

"He's smarter?"

"Yes! And remember, if you cannot be a lion, be a fox, cunning and wise. Shall we read a bit about El Cid. He, too, was weak. He had few men, but he defeated the more numerous forces of the Moors and drove them out of Spain."

"Because he was smart, too," Diego responded as he reached for the leather-bound book in his mother's hands. For a while, they read together, each one taking a turn.

Diego paused in his reading. "El Cid, like the fox, watched for hidden weaknesses in his enemies. Weaknesses he could turn against the Moorish conquerors."

"Yes, he did."

Diego continued reading aloud, his voice excited at his discovery.

CHAPTER THREE

Diego felt his frustration rise. For over a week, he had tried to find ways to spy on Manuel, but he couldn't. Every time he rode near the Gavilan *hacienda*, Manuel was inside, or out riding in the hills, or in the *pueblo*, or he simply stood staring at him with an infuriating smirk on his face. When Diego went to the *pueblo*, Manuel was at home, or in the hills riding, or, sometimes he would just glare at him haughtily from the back of his horse.

Today, as he rode with his father into the *Pueblo de Los Angeles*, Diego pondered his situation. The *plaza* was full of people, children younger than he dashed around the well in games of chase or mock battles, their gleeful shouts bringing a smile to his own lips. Until recently, he himself might be found among a group like that. The forces of the King of Spain were never defeated in the games of his imagination. Suddenly, his eyes lit up with sudden insight. It was so simple.

"Father, may I take some time to talk with my friends?"

"*Sí*, but I want you to be at the auction in an hour," Alejandro stated. "We need to buy new breeding stock."

"I will be there." Diego reined his horse toward the far end of the *plaza*. As he approached one group of the children, they stopped their play, and glanced up at him, wary of intrusion at first, but beaming with pleasure when they saw who it was.

"Diego!" Pedro Simeon cried out. "Are you here to join in our fun?" He was a dark-haired boy of about seven and a half years, whose gray eyes sparkled with mischief. He brushed his dust-covered pants off with equally dirty hands, a smile of anticipation on his lips. Pedro would play any game of imagination Diego could think up.

"Not really. I am attending the auction with my father, but I have the most marvelous idea for a game, if you are interested," he said. All eyes were on him.

"What is it, Don Diego," Pedro asked, his excitement causing his voice to quiver slightly in his excitement.

Dismounting, Diego was soon in the middle of the huddle of smaller boys, all of them listening with rapt attention. "Do you all want to be spies for the King?" he asked.

"Spies for the King? Oh, yes," came a quick chorus.

"What do we have to do?" Ignacio asked eagerly.

"Yes, Don Diego, how do we play that game?" others chimed in.

Diego smiled softly. "The King of Spain wants you to spy on his mortal enemy, Francis Drake. He is a sly one, very tricky and hard to follow. That is why he has to have many spies. The King wants the enemy watched at all times. He is cleverly disguised as one of us, so you must be very careful." Several of the listeners looked up from the huddle and glanced around the *plaza*, to make sure they weren't heard.

"Who is he disguised as?" Pedro asked, getting into the spirit of the game.

"Manuel Gavilan. That is why this is such a difficult assignment. Do you think you can do this?"

"Sí!" came the instant chorus.

"Now, I am the captain of the King's special guard. You must report to me. You must not allow yourselves to be caught. You can recruit others to be spies, but they must not be caught either. And above all, if you are caught, you must not give up any of the King's secrets," Diego admonished conspiratorially. All the boys nodded, knowing the temper of Manuel Gavilan.

"How do we report to you, Capitán?" one of the other boys asked.

"Whenever you see me, whether here, or at a *hacienda* or on the road, it does not matter," Diego told the conspirators. They were mostly *vaqueros'* sons, with the addition of a few *hacendados'* sons and *peons'* children. It was a wonderfully diverse group, and Diego sometimes missed playing with them so much that it caused an ache inside. This would be almost as good. "Ah, my friends, the King of

Spain sends you his greetings and thanks," he said with a smile and a salute, mounting and riding to the place of the auction.

*****

The reports kept coming in, sometimes when a *vaquero* brought stock to the de la Vega *hacienda*, sometimes in the *pueblo*, sometimes when Diego and his father were out visiting other *haciendas*.

"Manuel lays the whip on his horse too heavily," one spy said.

"Manuel had a crop laid across his back for talking disrespectfully to his father yesterday," another reported.

Diego found that to be interesting.

"Manuel ate fifteen whole chili peppers in only a minute," came another report.

Ai, that might explain his disposition.

"Manuel tried to ride his father's new stallion," one spy told him.

"And what happened?" Diego prompted.

"He ate dust," his spy answered. Both boys laughed. Diego kept that piece of news for future reference.

"He is afraid of water. His younger brothers were swimming in the pond on their *rancho* and he refused to join them. They called him a frightened girl. That made him mad. It was very hard to keep from being caught. I was trying hard not to laugh and in his fierce anger he was beating all the bushes with his riding crop," Pedro Simeon told him. "He finally became so angry that he jumped on his horse and rode away. The poor animal cried out in pain because of the whip. Perhaps the King of Spain will capture and punish his enemy for such treatment to a horse?" Pedro asked slyly, a bright glint in his eye.

"That is up to the King to decide," Diego finally said, not wanting to reveal any plans. Of course, he didn't have any yet.

The reports from his 'spies' kept filtering in, and Diego filed them all away in his mind. In the meantime, he visited Carlos, the head *vaquero,* each evening.

"Don Diego, when you fight, your eyes and your mind must keep working at knowing your enemy. If you do that, you will always be able to see when your enemy makes a mistake. Let your hands and feet take over the duties of combat. Come, let us spar a bit, so you can see what I mean," Carlos told him.

Diego wasn't sure what he meant, but he watched Carlos. After several nights, he said in exasperation, "Carlos, when are you going to show me something new, something I don't already know?"

"Diego, you already know all the skills you need to defend yourself. You always have. You just haven't used them the right way. You allow yourself to get angry, impassioned, then your eyes and mind cannot do their job and keep you from getting the bruises and cuts that I have seen you wear so proudly in the past."

Diego sighed. "Father told me the same thing."

"Your father is right, Diego. Listen to him," Carlos admonished.

Diego rode the range with his father and the *vaqueros*, read and studied with his mother, learned from Carlos and continued to get reports from his spies, although after several weeks, they tired of the game, seeing nothing new and seeing no results from their efforts. Several times, Diego had confrontations with Manuel, who seemed to delight in tormenting the smaller boy. At first, Diego forgot his resolve to be patient and hold his temper and came home sporting a bloody nose and bruised cheeks.

From then on, the boy quelled his fiery thoughts, finally taking taunts that stung to the core without comment, without action. But it hurt Diego to walk away from Manuel's disparaging remarks, his hurtful insults; he wanted nothing more than to shove his fist into the bigger boy's mouth and all the way down his throat. Instead, Diego continued to watch, listen, and wait for the right time his father told him would come.

CHAPTER FOUR

The day of the great fiesta Don Sebatian Gavilan held in honor of his oldest daughter's wedding dawned bright and clear. The dew on the grass sparkled, glimmering off the spider's webs, giving them the sheen of a summer rainbow. A slight breeze blew from the ocean, tempering the heat afflicting the area all during the spring. Diego could get just a hint of salt in the breeze. It was refreshing to him. He rode the dark mare his father had bought at auction and had given him to train. She was sleek, with long legs, strong withers and hindquarters, and a long, narrow muzzle. The Moorish influence could be seen in her lines and could be felt in her stamina as she ran across the hills. Riding on *La Vienta* was like riding the wind, thus the name he had given her. Only green broke when he received her, she had quickly turned into a fine riding animal under his gentle and patient handling.

"What is a *niña* doing on a fine animal like that?" Manuel taunted.

Diego's eyes flashed, but he quickly reined in his anger. He would continue to practice what his mother and father had admonished him to do.

"You should be riding my baby brother's pony."

"Father gave *La Vienta* to my care. I have been training her," Diego answered evenly, keeping his voice calm.

"A pity. Such a fine animal should belong to someone strong and brave."

"Point me in the direction of such a person and I might let them borrow her for the big race," Diego said with a smile, knowing full well that Manuel had been referring to himself.

Manuel's cheeks colored. "Such a fine horse is wasted on a mother's boy like you. She is better suited to me," he hissed.

"She does not care for those who beat their animals, Manuel. She would throw you in the dust as your father's stallion did," Diego responded with a slight laugh. Manuel's references to his mother continued to cause a burning fire in his heart, but again he practiced patience, knowing he would have his chance to prove he was no weakling, to shove Manuel's insults of his mother down his throat. Diego took in a breath and let it out slowly and evenly, continuing the exercise of control over his emotions and his tongue.

Manuel's eyes widened in shock at Diego's references. He rode closer. "You will regret those words, de la Vega."

Diego turned *La Vienta's* head and joined the festivities, ignoring the bully.

Later in the afternoon, the *vaqueros* readied themselves for the races and feats of prowess. One of the *vaquero's* sons dug a hole and loosely buried a chicken up to its neck. Its squawking protests could be heard over the bet taking and laughter. *Vaqueros* lined up with their horses and took turns racing toward the unlucky bird. The first two missed the chicken, which elicited boos from the watching crowd of *hacendados'* families, *peons*, and other *vaqueros*. The third, Carlos, bent way over his horse's shoulder, hanging on to the saddle horn with only two fingers. Down, down he leaned. His hands brushed the dirt as his horse's hooves thundered inexorably toward the unfortunate bird. The chicken was plucked out of the ground and held triumphantly aloft for all to see. It continued to protest loudly and flap its wings. Excited shouting and clapping accompanied his release of the befuddled animal, which ran in several directions before racing back to the pen where it presumed it would be safe.

Diego clapped and shouted at Carlos' display of riding skill. He must have the *vaquero* teach him that trick. In an enclosure, Don Sebastian was holding cockfights, and several *hacendados* had brought dogs to fight as well. Like his mother, Diego didn't enjoy those kinds of contests.

A commotion behind him caused him to turn. Near a pen where a small, but strongly muscled dog sat whimpering, Diego heard Manuel screaming in anger at a boy, probably the dog's handler, sitting near the animal. With each stroke of the short whip in his hands, both the *peon* and the dog cowered and cried louder in fear and pain. Suddenly a girl was at his side, grabbing Manuel's hand and trying to take the whip away. Diego recognized Rosarita and wondered at her willingness to incur the wrath of the bully. Manuel, in his anger, slapped the girl and turned back to the pair in the pen.

In an instant, Diego was at his side, reaching up and grabbing the whip. "Manuel, you have acted without honor. I challenge you to a contest."

With fury in his eyes, Manuel stepped toward Diego, his fists cocked, his teeth clenched. Diego stood resolute, even though fear caused his heart to hammer. Remotely, he wondered that Manuel and all those near him couldn't hear it. His stomach felt as though that chicken was down inside, trying to beat its way out.

"Diego de la Vega has challenged Manuel Gavilan to a contest," Carlos cried for all to hear. "What kind of contest, Don Diego?"

Diego wondered about that himself. What kind of contest? "I will choose one contest and Manuel will choose another. If there is a tie then we will let the *alcalde* decide on a tie-breaking contest," he announced.

"What will be your contest, Diego? A reading competition?" Manuel taunted.

Diego frowned. Anger burned in his chest, a fierce retort bubbling up, and sitting on the tip of his tongue. But he took a deep breath. *I won't give in to anger. I won't!* "If I chose such a contest, I would be taking unfair advantage of you, Manuel, since you have decided not to learn to read," was all he finally said. It was tempting to challenge the bigger boy to a swimming contest, but he realized he would be dishonorable in that, too, since his opponent was afraid of water. It was appealing though.

Manuel's fists tightened by his side at Diego's taunts.

"I had thoughts that on such a warm day a swimming contest would be nice, but since you seem to think so little of my riding skills, I will challenge you to a horse race," Diego said, getting satisfaction at the Manuel's reaction to his reference about swimming.

"My contest is a fist fight," Manuel told him quickly. "And since you challenged, my contest is first," he added. Diego just nodded and unbuttoned his shirt at the sleeves, rolling them up to a comfortable position. He handed his hat to Rosarita and stood calmly, waiting for the beginning of this fight that he had been anticipating and dreading, his fear warring with his eagerness.

CHAPTER FIVE

"You may begin at any time, gentlemen," Carlos said quietly. The *fiesta* goers had gathered around in a loosely formed circle. In the back there was the murmuring sound of wagers being placed. Diego saw a slight glimmering of fear in his mother's eyes, but in the eyes of both of his parents, he also saw pride and confidence in his abilities. His heart swelled as he also saw the love they had for him.

Manuel threw himself at Diego, pushing him heavily to the ground, wrapping his arms tightly around the smaller boy's chest. As the bigger boy squeezed, Diego felt his ribs creaking. *Ai! Focus. Focus! How can I win if I lose my focus?* His arms and hands were tight against his body and useless. His legs were in a position where he could not use them either.

"I have you beaten already, you worthless she-pup," Manuel taunted.

"Not yet, not while I yet breathe," Diego gasped out.

"I can take care of that," Manuel hissed, squeezing his arms tighter around Diego's body. The larger boy's arms felt like the shrinking leather bands the cooper put around his barrels. Diego's breath came in gasps. *Think, think!*

He didn't have the use of his hands, nor of his legs or arms. That only left one thing, Diego thought. Trying to relax and let his body go limber surprised Manuel and caused him to raise up a bit. Diego took advantage of the extra bit of room and made his move, slamming his forehead into Manuel's nose. The warm wetness of blood spread across Diego's cheek and the release of pressure around his chest reassured him of his good choice. Manuel jerked back in surprise, swiping his sleeve across his bloody nose.

Diego pulled his feet under him and jumped up and away from his opponent. "I have used my head, Manuel."

With a roar Manuel charged, the rage in his eyes was like that of an angered bull. But Diego jumped to one side, reaching out with his foot and tripping his opponent. Manuel landed on his face in the soft dust. With a growl, he got to his feet and rushed Diego. Stopping short of actual contact, he flung his hands toward Diego. The dust in each hand blinded him in an instant and Diego felt panic along with the pain of Manuel's fists in his stomach. His breath whooshed out of his lungs, and he fell to his knees. Diego tried to scrub the dirt from his pained eyes. He groaned at a kick to his side.

"You should have left me alone, *niña*. Now everyone gets to see what a weakling you are," Manuel's voice sounded close. The taunting burned in his ears, his gasping breath rattled in his throat, his heart constricted with humiliation. *It doesn't matter what I do, Manuel still beats me!*

"Use your eyes and your mind, Diego," he heard Carlos say softly from nearby.

How could he use his eyes, he thought in despair? He suddenly felt the toe of Manuel's boot against his side and a sharp cry of pain escaped before he could prevent it. *Think!* He heard the shuffling of the bigger boy's feet as he prepared for another kick. Reaching toward the sound, Diego was gratified to feel Manuel's ankle. Grasping it with fingers suddenly made of steel, Diego jerked the other boy's foot toward him. With a grunt Manuel toppled and fell heavily in the dust.

Diego rubbed his eyes fiercely, feeling the tears and grit mingle and burn his eyes. Rubbing some more gave him some semblance of sight, and he jumped quickly out of Manuel's way as the boy charged him.

"*Puerco*! Pig! Despite all your fancy tricks, you cannot beat me!" screamed Manuel, swinging his fist and catching Diego on the side of his head. Hitting the ground heavily, he watched the bigger boy's foot coming toward his head and he rolled away from the blow.

He heard Manuel's growl of rage and the heavy steps telling him of another rushing charge. In a move that surprised him, Diego rolled back the other way, catching Manuel off guard and tripping him. As the boy fell heavily to the ground, Diego pounced on him, reaching under his chin with his arm, making a vice to bring Manuel into submission. With Manuel's neck cradled in the crook of his arm, Diego squeezed. Manuel bucked and jerked around, trying to lose the tormentor off his back, but the smaller boy just clamped his knees on his opponent's sides and hung on, continuing the unrelenting pressure on Manuel's neck.

"Give up, Manuel. I have won," Diego whispered in the bully's ear. Manuel tried to buck harder, but his breath was wheezing now. The sweat dripped down Diego's cheeks, mingling with the dust. He squeezed some more.

"All right, I give up!" Manuel finally gasped. Releasing him, Diego stood up, smiling from the sheer joy the victory afforded. Manuel sneered at him as he massaged his throat. "I will win the horse race, de la Vega. You were just lucky this time," Manuel spat. Blood still dripped down his face.

Diego shrugged.

CHAPTER SIX

"After our contestants have had a chance to rest up, the race will begin. The course of the race will be to the edge of the pond and back," Carlos announced.

Diego was pleased at the declaration. That was a half mile. That distance was something *La Vienta* could handle quite easily. She was an excellent sprinter. He was confident she could win this race.

Walking over to a bucket of water, Diego was embarrassed to see Rosarita walking near his side, his hat still in her hands. "That was wonderful, Diego. You were so brave. Thank you for upholding my honor."

"*Gracias*, but it is not over yet," he answered, splashing the water on his face. He glanced up and saw across the clearing a Gavilan *vaquero* talking with Manuel. Diego pushed his suspicious thoughts from his mind. There were too many people, what could the bully do?

Splashing more water on his face and head, he rinsed the rest of the dust from his eyes. Someone handed him a towel. He wiped off the water and grime.

Diego sauntered over to *La Vienta,* untying her from the tree limb where he had left her in the shade. He led her to the designated starting line. She pranced nervously. "Ah, Vienta, you have so much energy. I am nervous, too." He lowered his voice. "I know you can do this."

"Riders, are you ready?" a *vaquero* called out.

"Yes," both boys answered in unison.

"Then mount and ride."

Both boys grabbed their saddle horns and flung themselves on their horses. *La Vienta* jerked, reared and bucked. As he fell through the air, Diego heard the mocking laughter of Manuel as the other boy's horse thundered toward the nearby pond. In chagrin, Diego wondered what had happened. His mare continued prancing and snorting, reaching around and biting at the cinch strap. Suddenly suspicious, Diego undid the cinch and let the saddle and blanket fall to the ground. A large burr clung to the fabric.

His indignation kindled, Diego retrieved the reins. Grabbing a handful of the horse's mane, he swung onto La Vienta's back. "Go, my beauty, go," he called. She sprang off in a leap that almost unseated him. Diego clamped his knees to her torso, leaning down until his face was whipped by her dark, silky mane. He bent down even more until his cheek touched her neck. Her hooves thundered with a rhythm of power and stamina.

"Go, *La Vienta*." He was almost halfway to the pond but noticed with chagrin that Manuel had almost reached it. "You can do it," he called out, feeling the wind whistling through his dark hair and caressing his sweaty body. *La Vienta* responded with a lengthened stride. One hand tightly locked itself into the silky mane, while the other held the reins loosely. Diego continued to call out encouragement, and the mare lengthened her stride, eating up the distance to the pond.

Manuel laughed as he rushed by. The bully had reached the pond and was coming back to the hacienda. *La Vienta* soon reached the pond, and, rearing, turned sharply and leaped into a gallop for the return. It disheartened Diego at the distance they must cover to catch up with Manuel, but he would not give up. "Go, *La Vienta*," he repeated, over and over. He reached down and felt only the barest film of lather gathering on the horse's neck. *You are a horse. A horse above all horses!* He believed his horse could ride miles before breaking out in a full sweat. She sped up even more, her legs a blur, the wind of her passing making his eyes water. Her muscles under his legs were steel, bunching, gathering and bursting with energy, generating the strength that made the ground rush by faster and faster.

Looking up briefly, Diego saw Manuel and his horse closer than he dared dream possible. The crowds at the finish line were shouting and calling out encouragement. "Diego. Diego!"

"*La Vienta*, you can do it. You can do it!" He encouraged her. Her ears flicked at his words. More power, more speed.

Her nose was even with the back of Manuel's horse. The bully was moving his whip up and down in a frenzy, trying to get more speed from his lathered horse. The horse leaped forward, but it was from fear, not the joy of running.

La Vienta saw victory, even with such a short distance left, and she leaped forward, her legs making a rhythm of joy and exultation. Her nose came up to the other horse's nose. Manuel reached over to lay his whip on *La Vienta's* withers, but Diego anticipated the move and jerked the whip from the bully's hands, tossing it to the ground as *La Vienta* edged just ahead of Manuel's horse and between the lines of people screaming wildly.

Halfway to the pond, Diego slowed the horse to a walk, allowing her to walk at a leisurely pace before jumping off. His *calzoneros* were damp with sweat, but to his amazement, *La Vienta* had only the slightest amounts of sweat gathered on her neck and chest. She nuzzled him as he took off her bridle, ignoring the cheers and good wishes of the people crowding around him. Putting his head close to hers, he murmured, "*Gracias*, my friend, *gracias*."

Snorting, *La Vienta* trotted out to the pasture with the other horses. She reared and called out, nipping a young yearling out of the way.

"Diego de la Vega, you have won the challenge. You have won it with honor," the *alcalde* cried out.

Rosarita handed him his hat, pride and happiness radiating from her face. He looked up and saw his mother and father, both beaming at his victory and the way he had won it.

"I remembered the fox, Mother. And this was the right time, Father," he told them as they enveloped him in a loving hug....

....Diego brought his attention back to the present, slowly pulling out of his father's embrace; his father, whose once dark hair was now steel gray. His father, who despite the coming years of loneliness, was sending his son away to learn, to mature, to bring the best of Spain back to his home in California.

"Return with honor, my son," his father repeated.

"I will, Father," Diego assured him and, pulling away, walked up the gangplank to the ship, starting him on his journey to Spain.

II . THE EUROPEAN METHOD

Introduction by Susan Kite

According to many Zorro versions through the past hundred plus years, young Diego de la Vega attended a university in Spain before coming home to fight oppression in the guise of Zorro ... or at the very least, had been away for a period of time.

Bernardo is a fascinating character and has been in most of the Zorro television shows and books as not only a personal assistant to Diego, but an important partner to Zorro. He even exists as a very essential character in the most recent incarnation of *Zorro* (2024, Spain). In various iterations, he is either Spanish, Indian, fully grown or younger, mute or not mute, or deaf mute.

In the original McCulley version, *The Curse of Capistrano,* Diego's manservant was a deaf/mute Indian. In the Walt Disney version, which style I write in this book, Bernardo came from Spain with Diego. So how did they meet? Their bond surpassed a master-servant dynamic. So how did that develop? *European Encounter* is my way of answering those questions.

I called upon my memory of a place I lived in, Heidelberg, Germany, and with research, tried to recreate a picture of the early 1800's. Köln is Cologne. Herr Fuchs is Mister Fox.

Enter Herr Fuchs!

EUROPEAN
ENCOUNTER

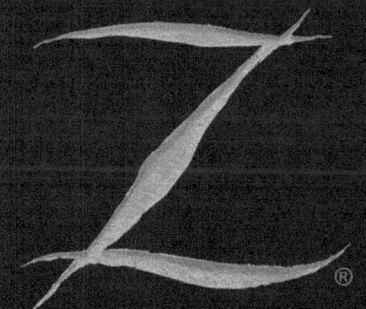

CHAPTER ONE

Chance Encounter

Europe — Mid-1819

Out of the corner of his eye, Bernardo watched the tall, young Spaniard standing at the rail of the ship as he sat, polishing his master's boots. The young man, although several years older than his spoiled employer, seemed more exuberant and fuller of life. Bernardo watched as the dark-haired man took in the sights and sounds of the city they were sailing into. A smile never left the Spaniard's lips, and it became obvious to Bernardo he was eager to be on this trip. The mute also felt he had seen the young *caballero* somewhere before.

The can of boot blacking slipped out of his hands and before Bernardo could grab it, the tin rolled across the deck, bumping against the young man's foot. The *caballero* picked it up, glanced around. His eyes met Bernardo's eyes. Smiling, he tossed the polish to the manservant.

"You are missing this, *señor*?"

Bernardo nodded and then pointed out his disability, expecting the young man to show pity and then retreat as many did. He had become used to it over the years.

"But you hear?" the *caballero* asked simply.

Bernardo nodded.

"Is your *patrón*, Don José Rodriguez of Seville?"

Again, Bernardo nodded. There was something about this young man drawing him.

"He's skilled with a blade."

Bernardo nodded and signed a query.

"Yes, I crossed blades with him at a tournament two months ago. I am Diego de la Vega, a student at the university in Madrid. I am very glad to meet you."

Now Bernardo knew what was familiar about the young man. As the man who won the Spanish championship, de la Vega was the only man to have bested his master. Don José railed against his opponent for days, claiming de la Vega had cheated somehow. Bernardo hadn't seen any kind of foul play.

But Don Diego exhibited no arrogance, only a natural dignity that Don José lacked. Bernardo was unused to that. Don José was haughty, barely looking at Bernardo when snapping out commands. You'd think he was King Ferdinand's son. For months, Bernardo had regretted the decision to enter the service contract with his current employer. The young pup was insufferable and intolerable. When this inter-European competition had come up, he was ready to take his chances and leave Rodriguez's employ, knowing full well such a move would make it difficult or impossible to get a position elsewhere. People looked upon retainers who abruptly quit with suspicion. They labeled them as unsteady and mercurial. Sighing, Bernardo squelched those thoughts as unseemly, since he was still in Don José's employ.

"I would like to know your name, *señor*. Are you literate?" Don Diego broke into Bernardo's reverie. As Bernardo looked up, the caballero sighed. "Forgive me, I didn't mean to be rude."

Bernardo shook his head. He could tell Diego didn't mean to be rude. Then Bernardo realized the young man thought he was illiterate. In a swift motion, Bernardo signed his proficiency in reading and writing.

A mischievous gleam came into Don Diego's eyes. He flipped a chair and gestured towards the polish. "Write it for me, *por favor*."

Bernardo couldn't believe the young man's audacity, but something compelled him to do as asked. As small as he could with his finger, he wrote 'Bernardo' on a slat of the chair.

Diego peered over the mute's shoulder. "Bernardo," he stated. "Now

I can address you properly. *Gracias*." Taking the rag, he wiped the polish into the grain of the wood.

Sudden footsteps caused Bernardo to act swiftly. He recognizd the steps and grabbed the rag from Don Diego's hands. The chair was overturned, and the manservant was suddenly polishing the next boot.

Don José Rodriguez came out of the deckhouse and stopped, recognizing Diego. "Bernardo, are you not done with those yet?" His scowl deepened. "Get out of here. Take them back to my cabin and finish them." Bernardo gathered everything in quick compliance.

"*Señor* Rodriguez, it is my fault your manservant did not finish. I pestered him with a few questions. His method of polishing is very proficient," Diego commented, forcing a smile.

Bernardo flashed Don Diego a quick look of gratitude as he snatched the boots and rags. *Don José is an insufferable lout.* He strode away with his head up.

"How I treat or address my servant is my concern, *Californiano*." He spat on the deck. "But stay away from him and me." Don José turned on his heel and stalked away, like an angry tiger ready to lash out.

***

In irritation, Diego watched the retreating pair as they descended to the passenger deck. Bernardo intrigued him. He seemed quick and intelligent, and Diego perceived a sense of humor rivaling his own. Too bad Bernardo was stuck with an intolerable lout like Don José as his master.

Seeing how close their approach was to the harbor near the city of Rotterdam, Diego decided it might be a good idea to go down to the cabin he shared with his teammate and finish packing. Out of deference to his roommate's higher social rank, when he reached the door, he knocked.

"Enter."

Diego opened the cabin door and walked in, halting when the point of his friend's saber held steady only one inch from his nose. He folded his arms and smiled. "Don Fernando, you have made your point."

Dropping the blade, Fernando Miguel Carroza y Arana laughed at Diego's pun. "Well, Diego, are you coming to the cabin to spar with me or are you simply here to open another book or stare at a chessboard?" Fernando asked.

"If we were not so close to disembarking, I would probably do a little reading, but as it is, I am here to finish getting my things together," Diego explained. Their easy bantering conversation belied a former rivalry.

Don Fernando was a first cousin to King Ferdinand, and at one time disliked the young *Californio*, who had, in a short time, shown an uncanny propensity for blade work. For his part, Diego had felt that Fernando flaunted his rank more than was necessary, until he had realized this was normal behavior for members of the royal family. The pair finally became close friends, and Diego had the privilege of observing the internal workings of the Spanish monarchy through his association with Fernando.

"There's a favor I need to ask," Diego said, while packing away his personal items in a large satchel.

"What is on your mind?" Fernando gazed at him with his head cocked, a gesture showing his curiosity.

Diego had never prevailed upon the royal cousin for anything remotely resembling royal favoritism, and hoped Fernando wouldn't take offense.

"This doesn't seem like something simple, like buying you a stein of local beer."

"No. Would you be willing to approach José Rodriguez about hiring his manservant, Bernardo? I know what he would say if I approached him with this offer."

Fernando laughed. "I know what he'd say, but I won't repeat it. He's hated your guts since that tournament two months ago. What sparked sudden interest in a manservant? And I suppose you are referring to the mute? Would it be that you want a hardworking servant, or in your case, you backward colonial, someone congenial? Or do you simply feel sorry for the poor man?"

Diego had a quick retort on his tongue but stopped before saying anything. He pondered his reasons. "Probably all three. I really can't say, except I like Bernardo's personality; he is not stuffy or condescending. He's very intelligent, too. I guess he's had to be since he's mute.

Would you be able to handle Bernardo's severance pay? I can pay you back when I receive money from home."

"Hmm, I suppose, but it will cost you, Diego de la Vega."

Diego wondered what Fernando had in mind as his friend stood there laughing.

"Study less, practice more with the blade. If you win the tournament, you'll have plenty of money." Fernando placed his sword into its case. "And you know you can win that tournament."

"I wholeheartedly concur, Don Fernando. For that matter either of you can win," said a voice from the open door. "Regardless of your wonderful talent, Diego, you must continue to practice. Expect tougher competition at this tournament."

"*Sí*, General de Silva," Diego agreed. He bid his mentor to enter and made room on the small bed for the general.

"Checking if you two will be ready to disembark soon. We will take a coach along a route roughly paralleling the Rhein River almost the whole way to Heidelberg," the general said. In his early fifties, the man was still agile and proficient in swordplay. His amazing skill in all aspects of fencing helped him earn his post at one of the most prestigious universities in Spain. He was among the best fencing masters in Europe.

General Juan Morales de Silva y Montez had intense blue eyes that could pick out the slightest flaw in the stance of any fencer. His steel gray hair and small trim beard added to the aristocratic bearing that was an internal and unconscious part of his being. Diego had found him to be incredibly patient in his teaching, and confident in the abilities of his students. As such, Diego felt lucky to have been chosen to be his student.

In height, de Silva was several inches shorter than Diego, but the *caballero* always felt he was looking up at the General, so powerful was his personality. In some ways, General de Silva reminded Diego of his own father.

"Hopefully, we will get to Heidelberg at least four days before the tournament takes place. That way, you can practice, rest, and get any travel stiffness out of your muscles," the general said.

The trip could have been accomplished overland, through France, but because of the strained relations between France and Spain, since

Napoleon had deposed the king some years earlier, they didn't consider that route. King Ferdinand regained power in 1814 but was still angry at the audacity of Spain's neighbor. Thus, the journey included a trip by brigantine sailing vessel to the Netherlands.

"Do not indulge in any undo pleasures along the way, gentlemen, specifically with the *fräuleins* or in the *ratskellers*." General de Silva glared at Fernando until the royal cousin blushed. Fernando was a ladies' man. De Silva also favored Diego with a glance. "And do not disobey the curfew. I want my team rested, not hung over and exhausted."

They disembarked and secured accommodations for the night.

The two men practiced for an hour and then Fernando suggested, "I think this would be a good time to offer to buy the services of an accomplished valet. I'm tired of picking up after myself."

"You don't pick up after yourself, anyway. But good luck." Diego paced for the entire time Fernando was gone. He realized it hadn't gone well when Fernando returned within a few minutes.

Fernando shook his head. "I think he would have thrown me out if I weren't related to the king. As it was, he refused my offer. He informed me he was satisfied with Bernardo. But Bernardo didn't look like he was thrilled with Don José."

"I think he may have an idea what we are up to, Don Fernando," Diego said with a sigh.

"We will try again in Heidelberg," Fernando answered simply.

The trip from the flatlands of the Netherlands to the Baden-Württemberg area of Germany was one of enchantment for Diego. The countryside reminded him of parts of Spain but was greener and full of low mountain ranges. The coach went up, and the coach went down in a constant motion, the only variance being that the mountains became a little taller as they approached the university town of Heidelberg. Diego's native California was also full of contrasts: flat, verdant areas alternating with wild, arid mountains.

CHAPTER TWO

A Momentous Proposal

Occasionally, Diego bumped into Bernardo. Both groups had paused in Köln and Diego took a little time to sight see before the sun set. As he strode into a small square, he saw Bernardo entertaining street urchins with a magic trick. Leaning against a building, Diego watched the joy passing from the Spanish manservant to the German children, without regard to the differences in national origin. After a while, Bernardo looked up, saw Diego watching him, and smiled a greeting. Then he borrowed several objects from the children—two wooden balls and a rock and began juggling. The children clapped.

A German police officer laid his hand on Bernardo's shoulder, startling him and causing him to drop the balls. The urchins ran away, leaving their property behind. Diego paid closer attention.

"*Wer bist du*?" the man growled at him. ("Who are you?")

The mute shook his head, not knowing any German. Diego strode over to the policeman, hoping his skill in the language would be sufficient for the situation. "Excuse me, sir, he is the manservant of one of the Spanish fencers. He cannot answer you because he is mute. He was simply entertaining the children."

The German nodded, scowling. "Advise him against loitering," he said before leaving.

Diego foresaw Bernardo's potential difficulty if he lacked caution. The political climate had changed in Germany, too, and some officials were suspicious of what they called alien influences. "Ah, Bernardo. Be careful. The official didn't recognize you, and of course, you couldn't tell him who you are." Diego sighed. "He said not to loiter."

Bernardo made a few more signs. In the meantime, a child dashed back and grabbed their toys, waving to the two men, and dashing back into the shadows.

"I certainly agree that you weren't loitering, but I guess the police around here don't appreciate talent."

Bernardo smiled and thanked Diego.

They walked back to the inn Don José was staying in. "I suppose I had better leave you." Diego paused, deciding to take a chance. He looked around and saw they were alone. "Bernardo, would you like to change employers?"

Startled by the question, Bernardo gazed at Diego. With a puzzled look, he gestured toward himself, then the caballero.

"*Sí*, Bernardo, I would like you to work for me," Diego said. He worried he might have overstepped his bounds.

Bernardo smiled, and nodded, then he gave a few quick signs.

"Slow down, Bernardo. You agree, but I do not understand the rest." Diego studied the mute's hands and facial expressions to comprehend. "Something about fencing?" Bernardo appeared impatient as he repeated the signs. He slowed down and repeated himself.

"Oh! When the tournament is over and we return to Spain," Diego correctly interpreted. "Very well, on the return trip home." With a smile, Diego left Bernardo and returned to the square. Both men were unaware that someone *had* observed the entire incident from a short distance away.

CHAPTER THREE

Imprisonment

Studying the small hand-drawn map he had received from Don José, Bernardo peered down the two narrow streets, angling out from the corner on which he stood. Although not a big city, Heidelberg confused him. Streets here felt more confining than Seville's, with the town jammed against a mountainside, a ruined castle standing as sentinel. After the experience in Köln, Bernardo felt paranoid about the possibility of getting into trouble with German officials and had not gone anywhere unaccompanied. This time, he could not avoid it.

With his map in hand, the manservant left the plaza, which was nothing compared to the Maria Louisa Park in Seville. Bernardo missed the Moorish inspired buildings and large open areas. Even Madrid was more desirable, despite it being crowded and bustling. This city appeared close and dark, making him eager to complete his errand and return to the university where the tournament would take place.

Bernardo also looked forward to the end of the competition, when he could terminate his employment with the Don José. That he had a position with Don Diego de la Vega eased his worries and made the idea of leaving the son of General Rodriguez a much more pleasant task. Bernardo didn't mind the fact that, technically speaking, he was going down in station, because Don Diego, being a colonial, was considered of lesser rank than the son of a hero of the Peninsular War.

On the contrary, Don Diego's offer delighted him. The young man's personality drew him in, and he felt that employment with Don Diego would be most interesting. It would be nice to be working for someone so congenial, too. The man enjoyed life and didn't worry about rank, position, or pleasing a demanding parent, as Don José did.

Bernardo refocused and found an error on the map. The road ahead of him stopped at a dark tavern. The map showed it continuing. *So which way? Right or left?* Like his previous actions, Don José drew the map while in a foul mood. *When is he not in a foul mood? Especially lately.* His employer had done everything except strike him, browbeating and haranguing him at every opportunity. Nothing Bernardo had done pleased his young employer. Gazing down the right-hand cobblestone street, then the left-hand one, Bernardo decided it looked friendlier down the right. More lights.

Now he had to find the residence of one of Don José's father's friends, a General Neufeldt, with a defective map. Walking up to a street vendor, Bernardo showed him the outside of the letter he was delivering, with the general's name and address on it, and signed his desire for directions. When the vendor gave directions in German, Bernardo realized his mistake.

Pretending deafness would cause the man to gesture the directions, Bernardo pointed to his ears and mouth. The vendor nodded and pointed and signed. It was easier to follow, and Bernardo continued down the narrow street. Halfway down the street, a loud clattering noise startled him, causing him to jump as if someone had shot him. Then a large hand grabbed him by the shoulder.

Terrified he was going to be robbed, Bernardo jerked out the tiny dirk he kept in his sash for protection. The individual knocked the knife out of his hand, and to his consternation, he faced the biggest policeman he had ever seen in his life. *Santa Maria! What do I do now?* Fear washed over him, and he began signing his intent, even showing him the letter he was taking to General Neufeldt. His captor grabbed it from his hand and, with an iron grip, propelled Bernardo toward the city hall.

Saints, preserve me. How am I going to get out of this? He was hustled along the street. and he soon found himself locked in a cell with several other prisoners. Sitting on a wooden bench, he pondered potential solutions and, coming up with nothing, Bernardo finally curled up with his back against the wall to rest.

Don José will undoubtedly look for me when I don't return. Bernardo picked at the food they brought him. Anxiety squelched his appetite. He shoved the bowl aside and lay down again. Later, he woke up shivering. Reflecting on Don José's behavior, Bernardo wondered if, somehow, his employer knew about his plans to quit and then hire on with young de la Vega. The shorter than usual temper, his hostility, and more demanding behavior had occurred just after the encounter in Köln. *If that's the case, then I'll never get out.* He put his head in his hands and prayed to the Virgin.

One of the other prisoners tapped him on the shoulder. Bernardo jerked up. It was an old man who tried to talk to him. He wore clothes that weren't too worn, but certainly not rich. The man spoke and it became obvious he had drunk too much wine or schnapps. But Bernardo realized he was being friendly, so he signed his inability to speak.

"Spanish?" The man asked.

Bernardo understood the German term and nodded. The man said something else, but he couldn't understand. Using signs was an exercise in futility, and they finally left him alone.

Bernardo dozed off again and when he woke up, he simply couldn't believe Don José would allow him to stay in jail once he had found out about his servant's predicament. His master's temper had to result from pre-tournament jitters. Paying the fine would make leaving Don José's employment harder, but escaping this vermin-infested cell was the priority.

A policeman brought in several threadbare blankets, and Bernardo took one and curled up again on the wooden bench. It took several hours before he fell into an exhausted, nightmare-filled state.

Another day passed, in which Bernardo alternately paced and implored his guards to get him a paper and pen. He knew that writing a letter to Don José should soon lead to his release. His cellmates had left; set free or transferred.

By noon of the next day, Bernardo finally encountered a guard who was more kindly disposed to his predicament and smuggled writing materials to him. He finished and slipped the note back to the guard. Bernardo nodded and smiled his gratitude. The guard assured him, in sign, that he would get it to Don José as soon as he could.

Then a sudden thought occurred to Bernardo. What if his master truly didn't care about his imprisonment? Motioning to the guard, the manservant took the note back and scratched out the name "José Rodriguez" and wrote in "Diego de la Vega" and the name of the building where the tournament was taking place. Bernardo felt assured that Don Diego would act and not leave him here. As the guard left, the mute heaved a sigh of relief and rested on the hard wooden bench until he grew weary and lay down again.

The following day, a police guard led Bernardo to a room resembling a courtroom. A magistrate and several officials discussed him; he saw his little dirk and the letter he had been carrying. When questioned, Bernardo could only shrug and sign his inability to understand the language and to talk. Finally, the magistrate looked at another letter and, glaring at him, pronounced what Bernardo could only interpret as a sentence. The only word which he understood was the name of a town, Berchtesgaden. Bernardo paled, having looked at a map of Germany before the trip. He realized they were sending him to Bavaria, a mountainous kingdom to the south, to serve whatever sentence had been meted out. Desperately, he tried to sign his desire to see a countryman, to get help, anything that would get him out of this mess. *I should have gone with Don Diego when he offered.*

Later that afternoon, the kind-hearted guard stated in sign that he had given the note to de la Vega's fencing master and was assured of its delivery. Bernardo's relief was short-lived.

The guard unlocked the cell and placed handcuffs on Bernardo's wrists. With regret, the German signed, the servant was being transferred to Berchtesgaden through Stuttgart this very evening.

Why? Why so far away? Why is this happening? Bernardo signed as best he could. Why was he going to Bavaria to serve a sentence.

The guard told him the big salt mines were there, although he was just guessing.

How could this be? What have I done to deserve this? Then Bernardo posed a query about the crime he was accused of. With a shake of his head, the guard informed him they had convicted him of being a spy and for drawing a weapon on a government official.

Reeling with shock, Bernardo leaned against the cell bars. The guard led him to the front of the building, where several guards and a riderless horse were waiting. As he helped him mount, the guard wished him Godspeed. Bernardo, understanding, could only nod his appreciation as the small group rode off down the narrow street.

CHAPTER FOUR

What Now?

Each evening before they arrived in Heidelberg, Diego and Fernando practiced their fencing skills. General de Silva was a hard taskmaster, but he praised their slight improvements each time they worked out. "Fernando, you have the makings of an excellent instructor someday! Not only are you a good fencer, but you quickly point out yours and Diego's mistakes before I can say anything."

With time and practice, Diego's innate talent flourished. "Diego, your fencing continues to improve. It is the joy you have for the blade, and it suits you well, but save your exuberance for exhibitions, not the tournament. Remember the rules of the tournament. You will be penalized if you forget."

Diego bowed. "Yes, sir."

"You could easily be a high-ranking officer in the defense of your homeland someday."

"Thank you, General."

After arriving at the small city, which their proud hosts informed them was home to the oldest university in all of Deutschland, they settled into their living quarters. General de Silva summoned Diego and Fernando to the tournament gymnasium, interrupting their plans to explore the city nestled by the Neckar River and mountainside.

The pair gazed at each other with looks of amusement, and then, gathering up their sabers and foils, followed their fencing master into the large building. After a brief but intensive workout, General de Silva finally granted the two young men their freedom, with the admonition to return to their rooms early in the evening.

Fernando looked sour.

Diego laughed. "Don Fernando, you will sight-see and meet the *fräuleins* at the conclusion of the tournament."

"As will you, Diego, your demeanor does not fool me for one minute," Fernando teased the *Californio*.

"*Sí*, but I have found no one who would appreciate the wild beauty of my homeland," Diego said in explanation of his aloofness in matters of the heart. "And I will be returning home someday soon, with no intention of leaving it again. I will find my girl in California." *Someone as beautiful and kind-hearted as my mother.* "But I, too, would not mind talking a bit with the Heidelberg *fräuleins*, when we are free," he added.

The pair enjoyed an evening in the local *gasthaus*, sampling a dish of fried potatoes and *wienerschnitzel* along with a glass of the local beer. They chuckled in amusement at the diners, who were already assessing the skills of those who were competing in the tournament in two days.

Apparently, the local citizens like to bet on sporting events here, as they do at home.

The next two days were a blur of practice and more practice, with General de Silva finally relenting on the afternoon of the last day before competition began. Diego retired to their room for a few hours of rest. Fernando shook his head in disbelief; "I cannot believe that you are going to take a rest when we have an entire afternoon and evening to enjoy the sights."

"I am older than you are, so let your elder have a bit of relaxation in peace," Diego quipped with a wry smile. Even his sleep was filled with dreams of swords and fencing tournaments. Despite his love for swordplay, he longed for the end of stress and drills.

"You are hopeless, but so be it. I will meet you in town later," Fernando answered, and left. Diego lay on his bed but, feeling restless, changed out of his practice clothes and started on a short sightseeing trip to the *schloß* on the side of the mountain. Passing by the inn where Rodriguez was staying, he hoped he might talk to Bernardo, but Diego didn't see him. He climbed up the mountain and found the old castle fascinating. Looking out over the river and town, he saw how the feudal barons controlled their estates with vantage points such as this one.

The tournament began early the next morning, and the early afternoon found all the Spaniards advancing to the next round of matches. The Spanish contingent faced challenges later in the afternoon, but all three advanced to the quarterfinals.

The following day, after two hard-fought matches, Diego felt exuberant knowing he advanced to the finals, but he felt sorry for Fernando, who lost in the quarterfinals. Rodriguez lost in the semifinal match, and Diego couldn't help but feel relieved he didn't have to compete against José Rodriguez, as he believed it would have turned into a grudge match rather than a sporting event. *But where is Bernardo? I haven't seen him at all.*

As Diego was putting away his blade and cooling off, de Silva gave him a scribbled note. Rodriguez's name had been scratched off and his name written in. "Diego, I received this during your last match." Thanking him, Diego turned away and opened the paper.

He blanched as he read the plea from Bernardo, who had been incarcerated in the local jail for several days. Looking up, he saw Fernando studying him with concern. Snatching up his accouterments, he motioned to his roommate, and they left together. "Fernando, we must go to the town hall. Bernardo was arrested and has been in jail for almost three days. I cannot believe that José would not pay the fine and get him out."

Within an hour, the pair was in front of a magistrate, listening to details of the arrest, trial, and sentencing. Diego was incredulous. "Claiming this man is a spy is ludicrous, and defending oneself when grabbed from behind is natural. As to the argument that he pretended to be deaf, how else would he get directions when he could not understand German?" As he became more agitated, his voice grew louder.

Fernando cut in hastily, "I would like to introduce myself, *Herr Burgermeister*, I am Fernando Miguel Carroza y Arana, the nephew of King Ferdinand of Spain," he lied. Saying he was a nephew to the king, instead of a cousin, usually got better results. The magistrate's eyes almost bugged out.

"Oh, sir, was the prisoner your manservant? Someone else came in and said the prisoner was *his* servant and that if he had been spying, then he deserved his punishment. He is on his way to Stuttgart with several guards. Nothing can be done now," he said condescendingly, slowly regaining his composure.

"No, he is not my manservant, but if you wish to avoid an incident with Spain, then you will write a note exonerating the man and someone fast to deliver it," Fernando hissed between clenched teeth. "The servant is a Spanish citizen and was not given a fair trial with adequate representation. Do you understand what I am saying?"

"Yes, your highness, but even for the king himself, I cannot pardon such a one as a manservant, who his own master has more or less declared a spy. Take that up with the servant's former master. When you get him into court, then I can order the servant returned for another trial." He showed the two Spaniards the letter telling of Bernardo's strange behavior, and Diego wished he had José in front of him now.

The Californio realized everything was directed at him. *José knew Bernardo's plans! Bernardo may have even told him my proposal.*

CHAPTER FIVE

The Rescue

Seeing no immediate solution, Fernando pulled Diego from the room and left the building. "Diego, I need to see Rodriguez immediately. Tomorrow, I can take him to the magistrate and resolve this. Let me handle this so you can concentrate on winning the match tomorrow with the Prussian."

Diego nodded absently, but when Fernando left their room to confront José, he acted without hesitation.

He remembered when he had acted against the bully Manuel back when his mother was still alive. It was her advice to be like the fox, cunning, wise, and strong, that helped him win that challenge. He could do the same thing here to save Bernardo.

Changing into the darkest clothes he had, and taking his saber, the *caballero* left the university an hour before the sun set. Remembering an incident back home in California, when the black colt he named Tornado snuck up on him from behind one night, he realized he could do the same thing to Bernardo's guards. With a chuckle, Diego remembered Tornado had almost caused him heart failure.

At a local clothier, Diego purchased a black cloak and a bit of black cloth. At the stable, he rented the fastest and darkest horse the man had. He inquired about directions to Stuttgart. There was only one road from Heidelberg to Stuttgart. Immediately, Diego took it, pushing the horse at a fast gallop, only slowing down occasionally.

Diego caught up with the guards and their prisoner after riding for a few hours. Tying the cloth around the lower half of his face, he pulled his hat down over his eyes and loosened his sword in its scabbard. Then he rode up to the last guard in the small procession and knocked him to the ground with his fist.

The man pulled out a pistol and aimed it at him, but Diego reached down with the point of his sword and jerked the weapon out of the man's grasp. Snatching it from the air and he aimed it at the two remaining guards. "Drop your weapons to the ground," he ordered. "*Schnell!*" he shouted, when they were slow to comply. They threw down their pistols. Bernardo gestured with his manacled hands, and when the fallen guard yanked Diego out of the saddle, he understood why.

The guard swung his fist, but Diego ducked, and hooking his leg behind his adversary's, knocked him to the ground. The snorting horses alerted him to the imminent attack of the other two men. Diego's sword flashed and the closest man suddenly had no weapon in his hand. Instead, he held his bleeding arm and moaned. The second man charged him, but the *Californio* sidestepped and knocked him unconscious with the hilt of his sword.

Pivoting, Diego was just in time to receive the solid blow of a fist under his jaw, the force of which knocked him to the ground. Dazed, he tried to get to his feet as the man grabbed a pistol and aimed it at Diego's head.

Bernardo kicked his horse, knocking the guard to the ground and causing the pistol to discharge harmlessly. Angry, the guard leaped up and jerked the servant from the saddle, hurling him to the ground, a blow of his fist sending Bernardo into a state of unconsciousness.

Crying out in anger, Diego recovered his saber. The German had drawn his blade and engaged the man in black. With a shout, Diego took the advantage and never relinquished it. The guard gaped in astonishment when, less than a minute later, he was standing with empty hands and the point of the blade at his throat. "The keys." Diego growled.

The man complied. "Now take the manacles off the Spaniard," Diego ordered. The German did that, as well. "Throw them here."

With the sword at the man's throat, he ordered the guard to put the manacles on and click them shut, throwing the key in the bushes. "Go to the roadside and sit."

"Who are you?" the guard asked.

Diego chuckled, remembering the cunning and sly animal that lived not only in California but in Europe as well. "*Herr Füchs*," he said, with a bow. "Enjoy your evening. And do not call out."

Diego checked Bernardo. He discovered a lump on his head and bruises. Picking the unconscious man up, he laid him across his horse as gently as he could and then mounted behind him, trying to ease the manservant into a more comfortable sitting position. Swinging the horse around, Diego ran off the guards' mounts and then cantered back down the road toward Heidelberg.

CHAPTER SIX

Aftermath

When Diego reached the university, it was several hours before sunrise. Bernardo was still unconscious, which worried him. Laying the servant down on the ground, Diego loosened the cinch on the saddle and looped the reins over the animal's neck. The stable master would hopefully believe a story that Diego had been thrown. Swatting the horse on the rump, he watched it trot down a street before he turned back to Bernardo.

Picking the manservant up, Diego carried him up to the room he shared with Fernando and quietly tapped on the door with his foot. His roommate had been waiting for his return. Fernando opened the door for him immediately. He stared in shock as Diego carried Bernardo in and placed him on his bed. "By the Saints, Diego, no wonder you are just now getting in," he said in a low whisper. "Let me take care of him. You go see the general. He has been worried about you, too."

Diego changed out of his dark and now trail-worn clothing, donning the workout clothes, and checked on Bernardo before going to de Silva's room. Dreading a confrontation with the general after having broken the curfew, Diego did not regret his decision to do so, whatever the consequence might be.

Diego tapped on his mentor's door, and the general immediately opened it, greeting him with a worried expression. The general's countenance changed to disappointment. "You realize that by breaking a team rule, you have forfeited your chance to win this tournament."

Weary from the fight, the anxiety, and the ride, Diego just shrugged. "General, you must act accordingly. Regardless of the consequence, I did what I felt was best. I had to act, because I know how much Rodriguez hates me and what he will do to get revenge against me. Helping my friends is my top priority. The European championship is worth far less to me than the needs of a friend."

"Sit down, Diego, you look exhausted," de Silva said gently, the disappointed look disappearing.

Diego complied, eager to rest.

"Fernando told me little, but I am assuming your excursion this evening had to do with the mute manservant and the ridiculous charge against him?" De Silva asked.

Nodding, Diego looked at his mentor for understanding. "General, I could not lay a great deal of faith in José Rodriguez having a change of heart and going before the magistrate. I had to do something."

"Diego, I envy your close friends, if you would do this for one whom you barely know," de Silva commented.

"But General, Bernardo is like a close friend. It's like there's a connection between us. From the first time I met him on the ship, he felt like a *compadre*, not just someone's servant. Am I making sense?" Diego asked, puzzled by his feelings.

"My impulsive student, I have been in combat and know exactly the feeling you are talking about. You are drawn to certain individuals, not just as friends, but as reliable people you can count on." Diego saw the light of approval in the general's eyes.

A knock on the door startled them. "*Herr General*, it is the *Polezei*, we need to speak with you."

Looking at Diego, alarm on his face, de Silva grabbed his saber and another near it. Throwing the second sword to Diego, along with a towel, he walked to the door and opened it. "How can I assist you at this unholy hour, gentlemen?"

"We must know if your students stayed in their rooms all night, Herr General."

"The contender for the championship has been practicing extensively with me throughout the night. His nervousness has kept me up far longer than I would like," de Silva laughed easily. The two Germans gave Diego a hard stare.

"Why do you check on my students?" de Silva asked. The policemen turned back to the general.

"A prison escort was ambushed on the way to Stuttgart during the night, and the prisoner escaped. The authorities suspected that the escapee's countrymen aided in his release, and they couldn't find this Spaniard. But if he was here with you, then perhaps our theory was incorrect," the German explained.

"Yes, perhaps your theory was definitely wrong," de Silva said dryly, as the two policemen walked down the hall and around the corner.

"Bernardo!" Diego exclaimed, rushing to his room without knocking.

Fernando glanced at Diego and calmly gestured towards the still sleeping manservant on his bed. "I carried him to the balcony before those two big lummoxes came in. I informed them you were with the General, which was true."

General de Silva entered and closed the door behind him. "Congratulations, my boy. You can play in the match today. There is absolutely no excuse I could give to disqualify you from competing without jeopardizing your freedom. And for this once, I am very glad." Walking over to Bernardo, he looked the manservant over, noticing several bruises on his face and a small lump that had formed over the mute's left ear.

While the general was checking him, Bernardo's eyes opened and he looked at de Silva in confusion. When he tried to get up, the general gently pushed him back down. Bernardo signed a query, asking where he was.

"You are in my room, Bernardo," Diego told him with a smile.

Bernardo asked for confirmation that Diego was his rescuer. The Californio nodded. Bernardo signed his thanks, before closing his eyes and falling back to sleep.

CHAPTER SEVEN

The Tournament

"Diego, you need to do the same, at least for the few hours remaining before the final begins," de Silva said.

"It would only make me lethargic. "I'll practice in reality for a while," Diego stated.

"The one thing I regret," the general said with a sigh, "Is that I have to accompany Fernando and José to the magistrate's office. You will start your final alone. I could wring that little popinjay's neck right now. If we don't follow through, it really will look like we rescued Bernardo and do not need to exonerate him. I know you can do this. You are an excellent swordsman."

"I will be fine, just so long as you can get that ridiculous charge against Bernardo dropped," Diego told him.

Five hours later, Diego readied himself for his match against his Prussian opponent. Although weary, adrenaline had kicked in as he limbered up and he felt the rush flow through his limbs like a river when given the signal to begin.

The Prussian was very good. His steel-gray eyes followed Diego's every movement, and his advances were lightning quick. After the initial greeting, the older man said nothing, his lips pressed together in a tight line. He scored the first point.

Focus. I can do this! The young man spun away and concentrated on his opponent, reaching in for a point. He missed the contact, frowning at his lack of energy. He remembered his engagement with the guards and his victory. Diego wanted this victory as much. The Prussian advanced and Diego moved back, careful not to step out of the circle of engagement. Their swords clashed together, and Diego pushed forward, finally scoring a point. It persisted, the continuous back and forth, circling in the confines of the engagement circle. Sweat rolled down his face, and Diego had to swipe his sleeve across his eyes.

During that moment, the Prussian scored another point. With a growl, Diego backed away and drew in a deep breath. *Focus, focus. Remember my lessons! Breathe deeply and continue advancing.*

He was growing tired, but Diego's inborn talent and General de Silva's expert training prevailed. Diego scored another point and another. When the official called the match, Diego had won. A short, stunned silence followed when the Spaniard was declared the winner. The Prussian was viewed as the local favorite. But applause erupted when Von Mannheim walked over and shook Diego's hand.

"Diego de la Vega, I do not wish to engage you when you have a few more years' experience under your belt. I salute you," he said in perfect Spanish, raising his saber in the air.

Diego returned the salute with a smile. "Señor von Mannheim, I never wish to engage you in competition again. That was the hardest match I have ever fought, and you are the toughest opponent I have had the privilege to cross swords with."

As Diego was placing his saber back in its carrying case, he noticed a small, folded Spanish flag, which he had not seen before. Pulling it out, he unfolded it. Diego assumed Fernando had placed it there this morning. When he was called over to receive his award, and they handed him a solid gold medal, Diego stared at it for a moment, unable to fully comprehend what had happened.

Then, holding the medal in one hand and the flag in the other, and with a rare show of exultant emotion, Diego held them both aloft and shouted, "Muestro Ferdinand y España. Für Kaiser Ferdinand und Spanien!" he repeated for the German audience. He wished his father could have been here. It was then that General de Silva and Fernando arrived and greeted him with a great deal of backslapping and bear hugs, saying nothing because nothing needed to be said.

When the men returned to their room, Bernardo was cleaning it up. Seeing the medal around Diego's neck, he beamed and signed his congratulations.

"How do you feel, Bernardo?" Diego asked with concern coloring his voice.

Bernardo pointed to his head and indicated a headache. Then he walked up to Diego and shook his hand, expressing his willingness to be his servant.

"I feel fortunate to have you in my employ, Bernardo," Diego declared fervently.

"Of course he does, Bernardo," Fernando joked. "He needs someone to clear a path through his room."

"Don't let his jokes alarm you," Diego quipped. "The royal cousin comes to visit me in order to see what a floor looks like. He has not seen his in a year."

"If these two quit bantering, you might be happy to know, Bernardo, that we have exonerated you whenever we find you." The general laughed. Bernardo shook his and Fernando's hands in appreciation. "It took a bit of arm twisting, but José finally admitted he had been hasty in his declaration that your 'questionable activities' resulted from spying, and your actions were probably only an unfamiliarity with local customs and language. He also admitted the defective map was his idea of a joke."

Bernardo scowled and signed he was glad to be out of the employ of the general's son.

"It would be terrible, though, to feel so much censure from a father," Fernando said seriously. "I have heard his father is always berating him."

Diego nodded, understanding how painful it would be for him if his father expressed any kind of disappointment in him. They had been very close before his departure for Spain. He missed him a great deal.

The more Diego was around Bernardo, the more grateful he was for the chance encounter bringing them together. The manservant provided a steadiness in his life and a comradeship extending beyond an employee/employer relationship. Bernardo appeared content in his service, too.

Life back in Madrid returned to normal for Diego, with his academic studies and military lessons taking up most of his time. Then, one day, he received a letter puzzling and alarming him, filling him with both regret and joy. It came from his father asking for his return home.

The hardest part was breaking the news to Bernardo. When he did, though, his manservant surprised him by insisting he would travel to California with Diego, if the caballero still wanted him in his employ.

"Wonderful, Bernardo. You will love California. It is beautiful and the señoritas are beautiful, too. My father's vintners make the sweetest wine. Father has the fattest cows and fastest horses."

Bernardo made a sign for a woman and smiled. He tapped Diego on the chest and signed again.

"Yes, I will explain to General Silva. Then we'll pack. We mustn't delay. Father wouldn't have written to me if it wasn't important."

Within two weeks, the pair stood at the railing of a ship, watching the city of Lisbon recede from their view.

We are going home!

CALIFORNIA
ENCOUNTER

CHAPTER ONE

Surprise!

Mexican California—1822

"By the Saints! This is too much to bear." Alejandro de la Vega's sudden outburst broke the peaceful atmosphere of breakfast. His fist hit the table and surprise almost caused his son, Diego, to drop the cup of *champurrado* he had been drinking. As it was, some of the thick, creamy chocolate sloshed on the table.

Alejandro maintained an ominous silence throughout the entire meal. Since his return from Europe, Diego had seen the signs of an impending explosion but was wise enough to let his father tell him what was bothering him in his own good time. Many things had been bothering him lately.

"I still cannot believe that we are not only receiving a *magistrado* from Mexico City, but they are sending a new *comandante* as well. Do they think we are a rabble of lawless cutthroats?" the elder de la Vega thundered. "Even as incompetent as Sergeant Garcia seems to be, he has done a good job. Why can't we keep being ruled by Spain? This is almost too much, this independence. The old way was fine."

"Father," Diego said soothingly. "We cannot change the fact of Mexico's independence. For another thing, even Spain sent *comandantes;* just consider Monastario. Maybe Mexico City can judge our leaders better than Spain did. And even you must admit, most of the time, Spain turned a deaf ear to our problems."

"Yes, I know you are right, Diego, but it is still frustrating." Alejandro had calmed down. "California has always been part of Spain."

Bernardo was taking away the breakfast dishes. Laying down the pile in his hands, he made signs for Sgt. Garcia and Zorro. Diego laughed in understanding. "Bernardo is reminding us that Sgt. Garcia succeeds mostly because of the intervention of Zorro."

Alejandro chuckled. Diego abruptly assumed a more serious demeanor. "Maybe this change in government will mean more stability and peace. Maybe Zorro can finally hang up the mask that he has used for the past, umm, two and a half years. Sometimes it seems it has been forever. A peaceful life, and perhaps a family. I doubt you have totally given up your quest for grandchildren.

Alejandro gazed at his son. "Perhaps you are right, Diego, my son. Perhaps this change is a good thing. Heaven only knows how much you have sacrificed and how much you deserve some peace. And grand-children would be nice."

While the two de la Vegas sat pondering the changes occurring in their part of the world, Bernardo indicated he was taking the carriage into the pueblo to purchase supplies for the cook.

"Bernardo, please find out if Sgt. Garcia has any more news about the new *comandante* and the *magistrado.*"

Two hours later, Diego heard the jingling of tack and the thud of hooves that told him Bernardo had returned. Puzzled, Diego walked out to the patio, surmising news of great import if the manservant came home in such a rush. He was right; Bernardo burst in the gate and immediately started signing.

Diego had honed his skill in interpreting Bernardo's signs in the past three years, but there were still moments like this one when he faced difficulties. "Whoa, Bernardo, I understood something about San Pedro harbor and a ship, but you lost me after that. Slow down." Bernardo complied and Diego interpreted out loud to ensure he was under-standing correctly. Alejandro had emerged from the *sala* and was listening.

"A ship from Mexico City arrived in San Pedro harbor last night, carrying officials from Mexico City. They will come to Los Angeles this morning, but you overheard a *vaquero* boasting he and several others will lie in wait for them somewhere on the route. You are sure?" Diego asked. Bernardo nodded.

"It would seem that some of our local citizens are trying to find out how good Mexico's money is," Diego said with a wry smile. Bernardo made the sign of a 'Z' and Diego nodded. "I will also make a quick stop in the pueblo on the way to San Pedro." Diego bounded up to his bedroom and into the secret room where he kept his accouterments. Changing, he took only enough time to write a hurried note, attaching it to a knife. As usual, when he donned the costume of Zorro, he felt excitement and anticipation.

Zorro then hurried down to the cave where Bernardo had just finished bridling and saddling Tornado. Signing *'Vaya con Dios,'* he stood back as his patrón swung onto Tornado and rode out into the mid-morning sun. The stallion's mile eating stride soon had the pair in Los Angeles. Sweeping through the plaza, slackening speed only enough to avoid running over the morning shoppers, Zorro threw the knife at the *cuartel* gate.

The weapon buried itself in the heavy wood, perfectly equidistant between the heads of Corporal Reyes and Private Montoya. Before the knife had finished quivering, the outlaw swept out of the plaza and galloped down the road toward San Pedro.

***

"Santa Maria," Reyes breathed, grateful El Zorro had a good eye. Reaching up, he pulled the knife out of the wood and undid the string holding the paper on the hilt. Reyes noticed it was addressed to the acting *comandante,* so he rushed through the *cuartel* gate and went to the *comandante's* office. The corporal understood that whenever Zorro left a message like this, particularly during the day, it held significance. Bursting in through the door, Reyes ran up to the *comandante's* desk, saluted, and stood at attention, wheezing.

Sgt. Garcia was working on his mid-morning snack, and looked up at Reyes in irritation, his napkin still tucked under his ample chin.

"*Baboso*, can you not see that I am busy? Come back, in say, ten minutes."

"But, Sergeant Garcia, Zorro left this at the *cuartel* gate, just a few minutes ago as he rode through the pueblo. He did not stop. It must be important."

Sighing, Garcia took the note and then read it. His eyes widened, and he read it again, his snack left forgotten. "Corporal Reyes, call out a contingent of six lancers, saddle your horses, and have someone saddle mine. There are officials coming from San Pedro this morning and they are going to be kidnapped by bandits. Quickly, Corporal!"

Garcia rose to his feet, and grabbing his hat, lumbered toward the door. Reyes pointed to his chest and looking down, Garcia noticed his napkin still tucked in. He threw it behind him as he rushed out the door. Soon, a contingent of eight soldiers galloped the road to San Pedro.

***

Zorro came upon an abandoned carriage about halfway between Los Angeles and San Pedro. Someone had cut the team loose and abandoned the carriage. Dust on the road revealed signs of struggle, but no blood evidence. Zorro searched for the trail the kidnappers took. The track leading into the eastern hills was easy to find. Even a child could follow it.

The hilt of a sword lay in the dust, the blade broken. Examining it, Zorro realized it was a Spanish-made item of exceptional quality. He kept thinking that he had seen a sword like that somewhere but couldn't think where. With a shrug of his shoulders, he tossed it into the abandoned carriage and rode up the trail at a slow trot.

When the trail narrowed to such a degree that Tornado had to walk, Zorro decided it was time to reconnoiter on foot. He motioned for the stallion to wait for him, and then slipped in among the boulders like a ghost. Although the bandits had left a trail any amateur could follow, the masked man would not assume they were so stupid that they would not leave a guard or lookout.

After perhaps a half an hour, he spotted a guard sitting on a boulder overlooking the trail. Slipping up behind him, Zorro put his hand over the man's mouth and jerked him backward off his perch. A quick blow behind his right ear rendered the bandit unconscious and, after tying and gagging him, the masked man climbed up on the boulder to view the immediate area.

Below him in a small cul-de-sac was a group of six bandits, most of them appearing to be itinerant *vaqueros*; he didn't recognize them from any of the local ranchos. Tied up and sitting near his position, with their backs to him, was the man he assumed to be the magistrado and an escort representing the Mexican military. From his best guess, Zorro figured the man to be a general. In shock, the outlaw realized that the Mexican government was very serious about this transfer of power, sending a man of that rank to Alta California.

"General, your government will pay many *pesos* to get you and your precious magistrado back alive," a slender man, presumably the leader of the bandits, told the officer.

"The Mexican government is not in the ransom business and will not give in to your demands," the general retorted. Zorro recognized the voice but couldn't remember where.

"Someone will pay this ransom. You are important. Someone will pay." The bandit leader paced. "Manuel, bring me the paper and pen. Quickly!"

"Sí, José," a smaller man said and digging in a saddlebag, brought the requested items to his leader. Zorro inferred these men were inexperienced and poorly prepared. The word 'inept' kept coming to his mind.

"Now, General, you will write what I tell you." The general shook his head, even before Manuel could reach him to cut his bonds. José's face reddened. "Obey me without delay!"

By now, Zorro silently laughed at this man's stupidity. He, the leader! Not having had a note prepared, not being able to write it himself and now trying to get their own prisoner to write something that they wouldn't even be able to corroborate as authentic. It was a struggle to avoid laughing out loud. Perhaps these men would give themselves up in frustration.

José was pacing and shouting again, and then he stopped in front of the general and, reaching down, jerked the man up by his collar. Shouting into his face, the bandit struck him with a backhanded blow, once and then twice, before letting him fall back to the ground.

Shocked, Zorro recognized the man. Juan Morales de Silva y Montez, his old fencing instructor! A thrill of excitement at seeing his mentor again, the man who was the closest thing to a father he had had in Spain raced through his body and he grinned. It appeared de Silva hadn't aged at all. He still had the trim look of a fighter, with an aristocratic bearing that even his present circumstances couldn't hide. Despite some more gray, de Silva's mustache and beard remained remarkably unchanged over three years.

Then reality set in. He was in the guise of an outlaw, in the presence of the man who taught him almost everything he knew about swordplay. Zorro may have been able to fool his own father for a time, as well as everyone in the pueblo, but he didn't feel he could hide his identity from the man who had examined his every fighting move every day for almost three years. He wouldn't be able to use his sword in front of de Silva, and he couldn't reveal himself to his former mentor.

Zorro believed de Silva wouldn't turn him in, but he wouldn't put an official of the Mexican government into that position. He saw José slapping the general once more. It was time for the man in the mask to act. Gathering his feet underneath him, Zorro waited for the right moment and then launched himself toward José. He hit the leader feet first and knocked down another bandit as he landed. José was unconscious before he hit the ground, and a well-placed blow of his fist took care of the other bandit.

"El Zorro!!" the other bandits said in chorus. One of them drew a pistol, but Zorro was quicker with his whip and had the weapon sailing through the air and into his own hand before any of the others could draw on him. Walking behind the two prisoners while holding the remaining kidnappers at bay, Zorro drew his sword and sliced through the men's bonds.

While re-sheathing his sword, two of the *vaqueros* attempted to rush him. One was shot in the shoulder, the other ended up with Zorro's fist in his face. Throwing aside the pistol, the outlaw concentrated all his efforts on defending himself. Out of the corner of his eye, he saw General de Silva contending with another of the bandits. Zorro slid on a rock, and he went down with his opponent on top of him. Zorro threw him off and ended the fight when he got his arm under the man's chin and cut off his air supply until the bandit surrendered.

Zorro saw the general had defeated his opponent and was studying him. "Well met, General...."

"I am General Juan Morales de Silva y Montez, and did I hear rightly? These bandits called you El Zorro?"

"Sí, General, at your service. And yours as well, Excellency," Zorro added, turning to the *magistrado*.

"Please, Señor Zorro," the *magistrado* admonished gently, "do not call me excellency. I am a citizen, like yourself, although most law-abiding citizens do not go around wearing a mask."

"My apologies, *Señor Magistrado*. The mask serves a purpose. I only ask that you not judge all Californianos on the reception that you received this morning. Most people in California welcome law and order; just laws and fairly administered order."

Surely you are not threatening us, señor," the magistrado said a bit testily.

"No, *Magistrado,*" Zorro remarked with a smile. "I am simply informing you I will not tolerate injustice, but if you are a fair-minded official, you will not see me again." Noise from below them on the trail told the outlaw that Sergeant Garcia was coming. When the corpulent sergeant arrived in the cul-de-sac and saw Zorro with the freed officials, he beamed.

"*Señor* Zorro, somehow I expected you to be here before us. Especially since I saw your black horse on the trail below. And you have saved us the trouble of having to chase down these rascals. It appears they are ready to go into the *cuartel* jail," the sergeant said brightly. "Corporal Reyes, Corporal Aguillo, tie these bandits up and make them ready for their journey to the *pueblo*."

Leaping back up among the boulders, Zorro waved to Sgt. Garcia and the others. "*Adios,* amigos," he called out with a smile. As he trotted back down the trail to Tornado, his smile faded, thinking of the pending confrontation with his old mentor. Somehow, Zorro didn't think de Silva would approve of the new Diego.

CHAPTER TWO

Disappointment

By the time Diego had returned home, changed into one of his more ornate outfits, and returned to the *pueblo*, the new *comandante* had just arrived on a splendid, dappled Andalusian, but General de Silva and the *magistrado* still hadn't shown up. Motioning to the barmaid, Diego ordered a glass of wine for himself and Bernardo to be enjoyed on the outside patio.

The *caballero* was more than a little nervous, and the manservant's presence helped to calm him. Diego had not been this nervous when he began this charade with his father, although he had not been happy with the deception he had perpetrated on him. Though Alejandro's disappointment was keenly, and at times, distressingly felt by Diego, he was also aware of his father's continued love for him. With General de Silva, whom Diego felt as close to as he would to a second father, young de la Vega did not know what to expect.

"Bernardo, General de Silva is going to wonder about your hearing impairment. I will explain you had a fever on the way here from Spain," Diego said in a low voice. He sighed. "I have a nasty feeling this may get ugly."

Bernardo looked concerned, which didn't reassure Diego any.

After Maria delivered the refreshment, the disheveled *magistrado*, along with de Silva, the lancers, and the prisoners, arrived in the *pueblo*. Sgt. Garcia announced the pair from Mexico as they entered the *plaza* and the entire group headed for the *cuartel*, where Diego saw them being greeted by the new *comandante*.

"Our new *comandante* seems to have a hard look about him. By the Saints, Bernardo, why can't we get a good one like Toledano?" Diego sighed.

Bernardo reminded Diego that Zorro had had to break in *Comandante* Toledano.

A short time later, the *magistrado* and his escort walked across the *plaza* to the tavern. Diego affected his most gracious demeanor and stepped toward the doorway of the tavern to greet his former mentor. "General de Silva, what a pleasant surprise." Memories flooded back, pushing secrets and deception aside. Diego was truly glad to see his old instructor, and the pair exchanged warm greetings, with much backslapping and laughter.

"Diego, you are looking fit, and you have also matured in the three years since we parted," de Silva exclaimed. "But surely you did not know I was coming and dressed for the occasion?"

"No, General, I did not know you were coming to California, much less our humble *pueblo*. However, I notice an official and the new *comandante* accompanies you."

"Oh, many pardons, *Magistrado*, *Comandante*," de Silva turned to the other newcomers. "This is Diego de la Vega, one of my best students in Madrid. Diego, this is Manuel Inocencio Hernandez, the new *magistrado* for this part of Alta California. I am accompanying him to the different *pueblos* in his district. And this, Diego, is Capitán Vincente Pedro Villagro, the new *comandante*."

The *comandante's* hard gray eyes looked Diego up and down. The thin, aquiline nose seemed to tilt higher before he spoke. "And what were you a student of, *Señor* de la Vega?" he asked disdainfully.

Diego saw the general start to speak, and he interceded. "A bit of military training, which, as you can see, I have not had the occasion to use here in our sedate little *pueblo*. General, when you have helped the *magistrado* settle in his room, perhaps we can talk together over a glass of wine. The local vintage vies with Iberian Peninsula and I'm curious to know why you came here."

Giving Diego a puzzled glance, de Silva said nothing other than to accept the invitation. "I also have a message from your old roommate, Fernando," he added.

The *magistrado* broke in. "I would suppose that many of you young *caballeros* would not have a great deal to do with the military arts, with El Zorro around to fight your battles for you."

"Zorro? What about Zorro?" Villagro asked loudly.

"A masked swordsman who called himself El Zorro rescued us from injury and death. For someone dressed like a bandit, he had the demeanor of a somewhat roguish cavalier," de Silva explained.

"I was sent to not only keep the peace in this area but also to capture this Zorro," retorted the *comandante*. "He harassed the *comandantes* and *magistrados* that Spain sent."

"Ah, but those *comandantes* and *magistrados* were corrupt and bleeding the people blind. The *peons* see El Zorro as their hero," Diego said evenly. "Neither you nor the officials who sent you know what has been going on in our *pueblo*."

"Nevertheless, Diego, I have received my orders and I intend to carry them out. If this Zorro is indeed innocent of being an outlaw, then he has nothing to worry about, does he?" *Capitán* Villagro said sarcastically. "The *magistrado* is tired after his ordeal, and I have work to do in the *cuartel*. Please excuse me, *señores*." The man almost clicked the heels of his boots together before pivoting and walking back toward the *cuartel*.

"I will let you two go. *Magistrado* Hernandez, I give you my personal welcome to the *Pueblo de Los Angeles*. Perhaps this evening you can both come to the de la Vega *hacienda* and enjoy our hospitality?" Diego asked. The *magistrado* nodded. "Until later, then, General."

Watching them go, Diego again felt dread wash over him. Bernardo tapped him on the shoulder and signed to him. "Yes, Bernardo, I forestalled any more embarrassing questions about my status as a student, and I suspect after Gen. de Silva becomes thoroughly disgusted with the new Diego, he will not have much to say to anybody else either," Diego murmured as they walked back to their little table.

When General de Silva finally came out onto the patio, Diego was still musing over his first glass of wine. Bernardo was off running necessary errands. "Diego, I am still curious about the reason for the fancy dress. You were never one to dress up in Madrid."

Shrugging, Diego took a sip of his wine. "General, there is not much to do in this part of California, and I have grown partial to fancy *calzoneros* and *chaquetas*. Tell me, what message did Fernando send with you?" Diego changed the subject.

"He says to give you his greetings, and tell you he has married and, I would suppose, by now, has a fine baby daughter or son to bounce on his knee. The *Doña* Perita was expecting when I left. I expected you would have married by now also, Diego."

"I haven't found the right lady yet. But I envy Fernando. I would imagine knowing him as I did, he is very happy. Who is this amazing woman who tamed him?" Diego couldn't hide the bit of melancholy in his voice.

Studying his former protégé, de Silva answered. "The daughter of Viceroy Pedro Del Marinta. She is very beautiful, and she has turned him into quite a family man." The general chuckled at the memory. Diego laughed at the thought of his former roommate, always known as a ladies' man, now a settled homebody.

"What enticed you to leave the university and become part of the Mexican government, if I may ask?" Diego asked in unfeigned curiosity.

"I desired a new direction for my life. My only son is in the Mexican Army, my daughter's husband has settled in Mexico, and there was nothing left for me in Spain," de Silva explained. "I am enjoying helping a new country establish itself. And I also find California to be a very beautiful and pristine country. It's understandable that you had no reluctance to return."

At that point, Bernardo walked up and tapped the general on the shoulder. When he saw he had de Silva's attention, he affected a beaming, childlike smile and showed him a magic trick, going through each motion meticulously. Diego understood what Bernardo was doing and was grateful. When the manservant finished his trick, Diego clapped and smiled back at him. Then he motioned for him to pull up a chair. Bernardo sat down between the two men.

De Silva watched Bernardo for a moment in abject curiosity, before asking, "Well, Bernardo, how is it you have not kept my young student on the right path?" De Silva asked. The moon-faced manservant just pointed to his ears and shrugged.

"On the way home, Bernardo suffered a fever and consequently lost his hearing. It also impaired his thinking a bit, but he would still do anything for me," Diego explained, when the general inquired.

"Please express my sympathy," de Silva said. Diego complied, giving a few signs. Bernardo just shrugged again and smiled.

De Silva sighed and drank the wine that had been served to him. "Diego, I feel you are playing word games with me. I must be straightforward with you." The general looked at his former student with a frown on his face. "I saw a great deal of potential in you when you were learning under me in Madrid. What happened?" De Silva's voice held a mix of anger, frustration, and sadness.

Knowing his mentor as he did, Diego prepared for the sharp bite of the general's tongue, the explosion that only occurred when one of his students did something incredibly stupid. "General, I suppose that what you saw as my potential was just that...potential, your desires for my future. Different desires than what I wanted. I enjoyed studying on the voyage back and that is what I have done since I came home. The military part of my training, I set aside. Currently, I don't want to use a sword." Diego noticed the general's shocked expression and then saw him transform into a poised snake. General de Silva leaned back in his chair, his face growing hard and his eyes becoming cold.

"Diego de la Vega, I did not train you to come home to become a popinjay, a royal dandy in a colonial state. I invested time in you, so you could become a courageous leader in this world. I would have been better off taking on Jose Rodriguez, instead of you, for all that you have accomplished." De Silva's words exploded like bullets, and Diego winced despite himself. He felt the same knife-sharp hurt he had experienced when his father had called him a coward. It had not become easier to take.

"General, please, there is no need to shout," Diego said. "I am sorry that I have not lived up to your expectations. I had hoped you would understand."

"I do not understand, Diego. It is like I am not even talking to the same person who I taught in Madrid. You are like a total stranger, a weak, sniveling court fool. Whatever happened to the courageous youth who risked everything to save a manservant in need?" he raged, and then he halted. "I have important things to attend to that will probably keep me busy until the *magistrado* and I leave for Santa Barbara tomorrow morning, so we cannot accept your gracious invitation. Good day, *Señor* de la Vega." Juan Morales de Silva slammed his chair up to the table and stalked off.

Diego noticed Don Diego's father watching from a nearby shop, anxiety etched on his face. As the elder de la Vega approached, Diego stood. "No, Bernardo, I do not wish to talk to Father right now. Please apologize to him for me."

Diego then dropped a couple of pesos on the table, pulled on his riding gloves, and picked up the almost empty wine glass to finish the last swallow. His gloved fingers curled tightly around it as he set it down.

Later, when Maria came to clean up the table, she found an extra *peso* on the table next to the shattered remains of the wine glass.

CHAPTER THREE

The Campaign Begins

Diego rode through the hills much of the night, his thoughts and emotions bubbling and boiling like stew in a kettle. The more he rode as Zorro and deceived loved ones, the more difficult it became to sort through his feelings. He understood the need for El Zorro, but sometimes his alter ego, the Diego that everyone in the *pueblo* knew, was someone he could not abide and wished he could separate from. That strange and ironic thought elicited a short laugh, and pulling up his palomino near a small, peaceful lake, he dismounted.

While the horse rested and grazed, Diego sat by the shore and skipped rocks across the surface of the water, listening in amusement as the bullfrogs dived underwater in surprise. The gentle sound of lapping water and the myriads of night noises had a calming effect on him and allowed for more peaceful reflection. As the first tint of dawn light started creeping across the eastern hills, the young *hacendado* mounted and headed home. The only regret he had was that General de Silva was going to leave the *pueblo* with an opinion formed from yesterday's conversation.

Diego showed up for breakfast in the *sala*, as he usually did, but didn't make any comments about his absence the previous night. As he bantered at the table about cattle and horse sales and the upcoming tanning season, he noticed his father studying him.

After breakfast, Diego excused himself and went into the secret room just off his bedroom. Changing quickly into the garb of Zorro, he dashed down the stone steps, two and three at a time, and saddling and bridling Tornado, was soon riding on the northbound road toward Santa Barbara.

Pausing on a boulder-strewn ridge overlooking the El Camino Real, Zorro waited for the *magistrado's* carriage to pass by. When it did, the outlaw followed parallel to the highway along the rise for several miles, unseen by those on the road. His compulsion to come was uncertain— maybe to see his former mentor again, maybe as a premonition of danger. But whatever the reason, Zorro had learned over the years that his 'hunches' usually were right in such matters, and he had learned not to ignore them.

Coming over a ridge, he saw several masked men in the middle of the road waiting for the carriage's arrival. As the carriage approached, the driver pulled the horses to a stop. "What is it you want, *señores*?" the driver asked.

"You carry tax revenues to Santa Barbara, and we would like this money. Our pouches are thin from the taxes we have paid, and it is only right that we get some of it back," the one in front retorted, waving his pistol. "Everyone inside, get out now!"

"There is no tax money," *Señor* Hernandez protested as he stepped to the ground.

"You lie, *Señor* Magistrado," the bandit returned and motioned to one of his accomplices to search the carriage.

Zorro dismounted and stealthily made his way down the hillside. When he was near the carriage, he loosed the whip at his side, and flicking his wrist, snapped it on the bandit leader's arm, causing him to drop his pistol. The other two brigands turned in shock. "Zorro!" they cried in unison.

Unsheathing his sword, Zorro tossed it to de Silva. "It is my understanding that you are a fair swordsman, General. Let us see," Zorro said, laughing. Plying his whip even as he ran, a second bandit found himself jerked from his horse and on the ground near de Silva. The third bandit swung around from his search of the carriage, took quick aim and fired, but Zorro threw himself on the ground, rolling. Then, leaping up, Zorro grabbed his assailant by the arm and jerked him from the carriage.

Zorro realized this bandit could use his fists as he dodged his opponent's blows. Finally, as the bandit rushed him, Zorro grabbed the outstretched arm and jerked him close, his free hand catching the man in the stomach in a close-fisted blow. The bandit went down, gasping for air.

Turning, Zorro saw the other two thieves closing in on de Silva and Hernandez with swords drawn. The general was holding them off capably, as Zorro knew he would, but the outlaw felt the odds should be evened a bit more.

"*Señores*, you are afraid to take me on? You engage older men?" Zorro taunted with a laugh.

"Do not speak so lightly of my age or my skills, *Señor* Zorro," General de Silva said testily.

"My apologies, General," Zorro said, as one bandit turned to engage him. "But I needed to say something to even the fight a bit, and apparently it worked," he added. "I meant no offense." His opponent made a sweeping slash in the air, which Zorro avoided easily. Ducking, Zorro reached in and grabbed the knife from his enemy's waistband, nimbly dodging away from the longer blade.

Zorro waited for the highwayman's next move. Thrust and parry, lunge, and dodge. The fight continued, with Zorro occasionally able to reach in with his shorter weapon and score minor cuts on the man's arm. Finally, the opening the masked man was looking for occurred and, with a quick flick of his wrist, disarmed the bandit. The knife held at the man's throat finished the fight.

Looking around, he saw General de Silva standing over his opponent as well, the end of the saber lightly touching the defeated man's jaw. The general looked at him curiously. Zorro helped him and the driver bind the three bandits and put them on their horses. "I will deliver them to the *comandante* for you, if you so desire, *Magistrado*."

Hernandez nodded. "*Sí, Señor* Zorro, and again I must thank you for coming to our rescue," the *magistrado* said.

"I sincerely hope that this time, your journey will be safe and uneventful," Zorro told the two men.

"As do I." De Silva's eyes gleamed with pleasure at their victory in the battle. "And, *Señor* Zorro, again I am indebted to you. Your sword?" De Silva was handing him the saber, respect showing in his eyes.

Zorro smiled and shook his head. "General de Silva, I know you broke your fine blade in battle. Keep this poor substitute. I have others."

"*Gracias, señor*, another debt that I owe you, as I felt I was not equipped to protect the *magistrado*, without a blade at my hip."

"*Por nada*," Zorro commented, handing him the sheath as well. The four men tied the bandits to their horses. Then Zorro mounted and took the rope connecting the horses together. With a wave, he turned and headed back toward the *pueblo*.

General de Silva observed the departing outlaw for a moment before climbing back into the carriage with the *magistrado* and resuming the journey to Santa Barbara.

***

The next fourteen days were a blur of activity, in which Diego had no time for self-pity or anything else, including sleep. It seemed to the beleaguered Zorro that the new *comandante* was determined to stamp out even the tiniest hint of crimes, real or imagined, in just a few days.

It began the same day Zorro rescued the *magistrado* for the second time. By the time Zorro arrived home, Alejandro had returned to the *hacienda*, incensed at the senseless arrest of several *peons* and a *vaquero*.

"What is that man thinking?" the elder de la Vega stormed.

Diego, who had taken the opportunity for an early afternoon nap, was curious. "What has *Capitán* Villagro done to raise your ire so quickly, Father?"

"One *peon* did not pay enough for his license to sell his wares in the *plaza*. Another protested the first's arrest. Still another *peon* could not pay for his bottle of wine. The innkeeper planned to let the man bring pesos tomorrow, but Villagro had the *peon* arrested. The *vaquero* became drunk and loud, so they arrested him as well. All of them will be publicly whipped before sundown tonight. No hearing, no opportunity for payment of fines, nothing! It is a travesty!"

"Calm down, Father. "I'll go to the pueblo and see if I can change our new *comandante's* attitude," Diego said. He too, felt incensed. Villagro might see reason and become more fair-minded.

"Zorro?" Alejandro asked. Diego nodded. "Be careful, I dislike this *comandante* and his arrogant ways."

"Of course, Father." Diego smiled his reassurance.

***

Zorro observed the first prisoner being dragged from his cell. That would benefit him. Some guards remained in the cuartel, but the majority gathered in the plaza. *Expecting me, the outlaw cynically pondered.*

Peering over the edge of the jail roof, he waited for the jailer to pass underneath him. When he did, Zorro dropped on the guard's shoulders, dragging him to the ground and swiftly putting a hand over the man's mouth to prevent an outcry. After the hilt of his knife had rendered the guard unconscious, the outlaw dug for the keys to the cells. He opened the doors and motioned for the prisoners to hide in the stables.

With utmost silence, Zorro approached the remaining three soldiers in the *cuartel* from behind while they were trying to see the whippings through a slit in the *cuartel* door. He knocked them unconscious in quick succession. One *peon* approached from the stable.

"*Señor* Zorro," he whispered. "We will drag these into the cells. Rescue Manuel, *por favor*." The masked man nodded and after instructing them to escape over the back wall when they finished, he ran up the stairs to the second story barracks. Climbing onto the roof, he had an excellent view of the *plaza*. Jumping down to the *cuartel* wall, Zorro unlimbered his whip. Just as the soldier was drawing back his arm to begin Manuel's punishment, the outlaw did the same and the end of his whip curled around the soldier's upraised arm, jerking him off balance and causing him to drop his whip.

"*Comandante*, a man who has forgotten to bring enough *pesos* to pay for his wine, does not deserve this kind of punishment, but the man who orders it does." Zorro leaped down next to Villagro and jerked him close to his body. His knife almost magically found its way into his left hand and under the *comandante's* chin.

"I am a fair man, *Capitán* Villagro. I would suggest that you be the same and I will not have occasion to do more with this knife than threaten you with it," Zorro hissed in the *comandante's* ear.

"Sgt. Garcia, cut the prisoner loose," he said, more loudly. Garcia was quick to comply with the outlaw's orders, and the *peon* ran down a dark street. "The rest of you back up quickly."

Then Zorro whistled and the thundering hooves of the great black stallion reverberated in the *plaza*. "Get on the horse, *Comandante*."

As soon as Villagro had mounted, Zorro swung on behind him, and with a shout, wheeled Tornado around, and galloped away. As soon as he reached the end of the *plaza*, he gave the *capitán* a shove and threw him ignominiously into the dust. Zorro's laugh echoed down the dark streets.

CHAPTER FOUR

Villagro Sets His Snares

If anything, Zorro's action seemed to spur Villagro to even greater action against the citizenry of the *pueblo*. For a two-week period, there was almost no moment of respite for El Zorro. A *peon* threw a mud clod against the *cuartel* gates; Villagro set his execution for that evening. The owner of a small *rancho* protested the advances of a soldier to his only daughter. They sentenced him to work in the tin mines north of Los Angeles. Another *peon* laughed at a soldier; the *comandante* sentenced him to be whipped. The incidents continued almost without ceasing. Zorro rode to their rescue.

Eventually, there were more fugitives from justice than there were free citizens. The most recent incident occurred when a *vaquero's* horse was spooked in the *plaza* and knocked down several soldiers. They fined the *vaquero* one hundred pesos.

To Alejandro, it seemed endless. He didn't even tell his son about the latest incident with the *vaquero*. He and Bernardo had left him dozing in the library, while they rode into the *pueblo* and handed the hundred *pesos* over to the *comandante*. Villagro didn't look pleased and argued with the elder de la Vega.

"But to pay so much for an itinerant *vaquero*, Don Alejandro," Villagro protested.

"Did you or did you not set the fine at one hundred *pesos*?" Alejandro retorted.

"I did," the *comandante* answered, frowning.

The old man calmly said, "Here are the hundred pesos." It was a struggle to remain calm in front of the *capitán*.

"Very well, *Señor* de la Vega," Villagro said, disappointment in his voice. "Sgt. Garcia, release the *vaquero* José Braconos. His fine has been paid."

"Wonderful, *Comandante*...," Garcia beamed until he saw the sour look on Villagro's face. He saluted, then carried out the order.

"Good day, *Comandante*," Alejandro said curtly and followed Sgt. Garcia out the door.

Later that morning, soldiers forced a *peon* family from their home at gunpoint. They accused the father of stealing cattle from a nearby *rancho*. The father protested that the steer had only wandered onto his small plot of land, and the peon was subsequently pistol whipped and carried off to the *cuartel* jail. His wife and three children could only look on in anguish and pray that God would deliver them from this horror.

The oldest boy ran to the nearby *hacienda* and asked for help, since it was the rancher's steer. Disturbed by the event, the rancher rode to see his friend, Alejandro de la Vega.

"Alejandro, what can I do? I came here to ask your advice before going into the *cuartel* to inform *Capitán* Villagro of his mistake in the arrest of Jorge Melendez," Antonio Briales asked in consternation. "I do not believe that even Zorro can continue to keep up with all of this deviltry Villagro seems capable of thinking up."

Alejandro frowned and pulled at his beard. "Let us both go into the *pueblo,* and you can explain the mistake, Antonio, my friend. Perhaps this situation will not even need the help of Zorro," he said, with a tight smile, hoping that he was right. He was worried about Diego, and realized Antonio was correct in his assessment. In fact, an ugly thought crossed his mind; that Villagro's main purpose in being in the *pueblo* wasn't to bring law and order to Los Angeles, but to kill or capture Zorro.

Sudden inspiration caused him to smile more broadly. "Antonio, we might get help from another direction. I remember the *magistrado* saying that he would be returning to the area in about two weeks, stopping at San Gabriel to worship and to admire the fine architecture of the mission. I will send a servant with a note informing him of the happenings here. He struck me as a fair-minded individual."

"Wonderful idea, Alejandro! We certainly can be no worse off."

Taking a few minutes, Alejandro crafted a succinct but well-worded letter. Then he gave it to Bernardo, charging him to hand it only to the *magistrado* or the general. Bernardo wasted no time, being concerned about the unfolding events as well.

As Bernardo was riding off, Diego came into the *sala*, yawning. "Father, why is Bernardo riding off so hastily?"

"I hope that the new *magistrado* is following his planned itinerary he had mentioned to me the evening before his departure to Santa Barbara. I wrote a note to Señor Hernandez, informing him of these outrages in our pueblo and expressing my hope that he will come speedily, before anyone else is unjustly punished or before Villagro kills or captures Zorro. You understand, that's his purpose here."

Diego nodded, recalling the brief conversation with the *comandment* two weeks before. Now everything made sense. He had been too busy and too tired freeing prisoners and eluding the ever-increasing patrols to remember. Diego mentioned the comment Villagro had made when he had first met him.

"You look tired, Diego," Antonio observed.

"Too much reading and composing, Don Antonio," Diego said with a slight smile. "Nothing that a little fresh air and a bit of rest would not cure." Seeing his father donning his riding gloves, he inquired, "Riding into the *pueblo*, Father?"

"*Sí*, my son. It seems Antonio's neighbor was arrested for having one of the Briales' steers on his property. We are talking to the *comandmente*," Alejandro explained.

"Be careful of walking in tall grass where snakes lurk," Diego enigmatically warned. "You can't see them until their fangs are in your ankle."Alejandro nodded, knowing what Diego was referring to.

Once the men departed, Diego proceeded to his bedroom and entered the secret chamber. There, he transformed into Zorro. Knowing his father's hot temper, the masked man was going to keep a close eye on these developments. He had a bad feeling.

***

Villagro's aide, a man whose name was Corporal Manolito Duarte, admitted Alejandro and Antonio into the *comandante's* office. But no one called him Corporal Duarte. By his own insistence, and at the point of a gun or the end of a sword, Duarte had convinced everyone in and around the *pueblo* that he was to be called Corporal *Diablo.* The *peons* said that; indeed, he was a devil. His cruelty was unrivaled, and he was a master of weaponry. Whenever he walked by, many of the local folk made the sign of the cross. This suited his purposes perfectly.

"What can I do for you, *señores*?" Villagro asked in a bored manner.

"Comandante," Antonio Briales said, "they took one of my neighbors to the *cuartel* and accused him of being a cattle thief. That is a false accusation. The steer wandered onto his plot of land, as is common for cattle in California. The man is innocent."

"We have already gotten a confession from him," Villagro stated evenly.

"A confession obtained by brute force and cruel torture, no doubt," Alejandro retorted.

"Corporal *Diablo,* arrest Don Alejandro de la Vega for treasonous slander against a representative of the Mexican government. And escort Don Antonio out of the *cuartel.*"

"No, you cannot do this, *comandante*," Briales cried in disbelief.

"I can and I …."

Villagro's statement was unfinished, when Zorro burst through the door from his private quarters.

Zorro!" Villagro shouted in astonishment at the audacity of the outlaw. He drew his sword.

"Comandante, you have been a major annoyance to the people of this *pueblo*, and especially to me. I will tolerate no more," Zorro thundered and attacked with a drawn sword.

Zorro realized the *comandante* was very good, almost as good as himself, but his primary concern was Corporal *Diablo.* Out of the corner of his eye, he noticed the soldier trying to shoot him. Keeping Villagro between himself and the corporal, he fought a battle, which he felt would be to the death; his, if he didn't find some way to neutralize *Diablo.*

"*Señores*, leave us," Zorro said. "This is between me and the *comandante*."

Instead of leaving, Alejandro leaped for *Diablo*. Grabbing the pistol, Alejandro jerked it down just as it discharged. The ball gouged a furrow across the elder de la Vega's leg, causing his collapse to the floor.

Antonio swiftly joined his friend. "*Señor* Briales, get *Señor* de la Vega out of here and to a doctor," Zorro ordered, still battling Villagro, but with a determined set to his features. The *comandante* lunged and Zorro found the opening that he needed. Leaping to one side, his blade went into Villagro's sword arm, the force of the thrust breaking the outlaw's sword and the *comandante's* arm.

Zorro realized he had fought in anger when he saw the force with which the saber entered its target, something he was taught should never be done.

Diablo leaped at him with a drawn knife and Zorro danced to one side, tripping him with his foot. Picking up the corporal by the collar of his uniform, and before the soldier could collect himself, Zorro threw him against the wall. *Diablo* collapsed without a sound.

Turning back to the *comandante*, he gave his warning. "*Comandante*, I would suggest that you request a change of assignments. Los Angeles is getting too dangerous for you. I should have killed you, but I will give you a chance to bow out with honor. If you so much as think of harassing the people of this *pueblo* again to capture me, I will come and finish the job I started today. I hope you understand me clearly, *Capitán* Villagro."

Zorro left in the same manner he entered.

Only after did Villagro think of seeking help.

***

General de Silva read Alejandro de la Vega's note with great concern. He realized that someone must have promised Villagro a great deal of money to capture or kill Zorro. The purpose of the attacks on Los Angeles citizens was clear. Don Alejandro hinted but didn't directly state it. Motioning to Bernardo to sit down, the general took the note into the *magistrado*.

"This is an outrage, Juan, an absolute outrage. We must go back to

Los Angeles immediately and confront Villagro with this," Hernandez blustered.

"We must also be wary, though. Apparently, there is someone in Mexico City who is secretly working behind the scenes. We were not told of any vendettas against Zorro," de Silva reminded the *magistrado*.

"You are right. General, what is your opinion on the cause?" Hernandez asked. "Why didn't they pardon Zorro during the government change, like they did with others?"

Probably because Zorro is a patriot of California, not Spain or Mexico. He has not been working to overthrow Spanish rule, but to see that justice is rendered to all citizens of the area. He may have caused the downfall of a Spanish *comandante*, but he also caused the downfall of one who was fighting against the Spanish rule. Zorro's actions are not political. I would imagine that he raised the ire of more than one Mexican official the past couple of years."

"You speak as though you have a great deal of respect for this outlaw, General," Hernandez said, looking intently at de Silva.

"Our government, army, and people need patriots like him. And this Zorro reminds me of someone I once knew," de Silva said thoughtfully.

"We must still go to Los Angeles. My orders were to have Zorro captured, if possible, and brought to trial, and I am the *magistrado* of this region. I intend to enforce the directives given to me."

"And I outrank Villagro and have the authority along with you to strip him of his post and his rank for his unjust tyranny against the citizens of Los Angeles," de Silva said. "You are right. We need to go to Los Angeles immediately."

CHAPTER FIVE

Diablo Plots Revenge

When they arrived, Bernardo followed the two officials into the *comandante's* office and stood at the little window, presumably preoccupied with activities on the parade ground. However, his mind remained focused on the conversation behind him."

"We have received a letter detailing all of your activities for the past two weeks, *Comandante*." Hernandez waved the letter in front of Villagro's face. "Would you care to explain the reasoning for this tyrannical behavior?"

"The people here are rebellious, that infernal outlaw has influenced them. They do not obey the laws, are treasonous and disrespectful, and defiant of the rule of Mexico City," Villagro said evenly, his mouth set in a hard line. "I was told to capture or preferably, kill the outlaw, and that is what I was trying to do."

"Apparently the Fox is smarter than you are, *Capitán* Villagro," de Silva said with a smile. "He also seems to have a better sense of justice."

"The Mexican government also sent me," Hernandez added. "Nevertheless, I received orders to administer justice, and that includes El Zorro. He is to be captured if possible and brought to trial. I will find out who is giving you your orders and he, too, will come to trial. I came here with no intention of being a puppet administrator, and I will allow no one to undermine my authority. Villagro, you are finished in California." The *magistrado* regained his composure.

"I am a general in the Mexican army, while you are a *capitán*. I hereby strip you of your rank and position, pending a thorough investigation," de Silva stated formally. "Sgt. Garcia," he shouted, knowing that the corpulent sergeant was just outside the door.

Garcia entered the room and saluted. "Yes, General."

"I am assigning you to act under my command until a new comandante is appointed for this cuartel. I am charging you with the responsibility of posting a guard outside of *Señor* Villagro's room. He is under house arrest. The *magistrado* and I will take rooms at the inn, and I will visit the de la Vega *hacienda* later on this evening," he informed the sergeant.

"Oh, *sí*, General de Silva." Garcia smiled and saluted. He looked relieved.

"By the way, Villagro, how did you hurt your arm?" The general asked, having noticed the bound and splinted appendage as soon as he had walked into the room.

"That cursed Zorro attacked me while I was making an arrest," Villagro returned.

De Silva laughed. Noticing Bernardo, he quickly jotted down a note and handed it to the manservant. Glancing at it, Bernardo nodded and left.

***

Zorro watched from the dark doorway of a side room as the doctor cleaned and bandaged his father's wound. "You are fortunate, Don Alejandro, that this was only a glancing wound. Take this cane and stay off your feet as much as you can for the next several days. That will give the wound time to close and heal," the physician admonished Alejandro.

Don Antonio helped his friend to his carriage, and they rode out of the *pueblo*. More than Zorro watched the men leaving.

"*Señores*, if you do not mind, I will accompany you to the de la Vega *hacienda*," Zorro said as he rode up alongside the carriage. "Señor de la Vega, thank you for your help in the comandante's office. I am only sorry that you were injured."

"It was the least I could do to help you after all you have done the past," Alejandro replied. Zorro rode with them until they were almost to the *hacienda* and then he left them. Diego emerged from the library to investigate the commotion as Don Antonio and a servant assisted Alejandro to the guest room.

"Father, what happened?" Diego cried.

"Just a slight wound trying to help Zorro," Alejandro answered nonchalantly. "But the doctor ordered me to stay off of it."

"Father, leave the derring-do to Zorro," Diego chided him. Turning to *Señor* Briales, he said, "Don Antonio, would you like a glass of wine?

"No, Diego, I must get home. My wife will wonder what has become of me, but *gracias*." Briales took his leave.

"Father, I almost had heart failure when that pistol went off. You should not have taken such a chance," Diego said, when they were alone.

"Do not lecture a father on how he should or should not protect his child," Alejandro said a bit testily. His leg had begun to ache.

A knock came at the door. "Enter," both men said together. Bernardo entered with a note from the general. Handing it to Diego, he signed to show what had happened at the *comandante's* office.

"Wonderful! They ousted Villagro from office!" Alejandro exclaimed. "Once again, everything will return to normal."

"Bernardo, did the general say anything about coming out here in front of *Capitán* Villagro?" Diego asked. Bernardo nodded.

"What is wrong, son?" Alejandro asked, seeing the concern on Diego's face.

"Villagro was not working alone," Diego explained. "There are soldiers who gladly do his bidding. Although Villagro is powerless and in custody, I believe he will seek revenge. I am going out to monitor things. You will have to explain my absence any way that you see fit."

"Assist me to the sala where there is more space to entertain guests. I can recline on the settee against some pillows," Alejandro told them. As soon as he was settled, Diego slipped through the entrance to the secret cave and changed his outfit. Mounting Tornado, Zorro rode out into the twilight. Underneath him, even Tornado felt tired.

***

Diablo seethed at the indignities heaped on his *comandante*. He would have to act, and perhaps *Capitán* Villagro would reward him with a promotion later. He watched as Don Antonio and Don Alejandro rode out of the *pueblo*.

He sauntered back to his tiny room and detailed his plan to three other soldiers who were faithful to the *capitán*. Together, the quintet would sweep away anyone who got in their way, starting with Gen. de Silva, Zorro — and down the list to that fat idiot, Garcia.

Changing into the garb of *vaqueros*, the four men mounted and rode out of the pueblo toward the de la Vega *hacienda*. Rubbing the bump on his head, *Diablo* thought what pleasure it would be to kill Zorro, if not tonight, then later.

***

An hour after the confrontation with the *comandante*, de Silva borrowed a horse from the stable master and rode out to the de la Vega *hacienda*. Corporal Reyes and Private Ortega accompanied him at Sgt. Garcia's insistence. The *magistrado*, pleading fatigue, stayed in his room at the inn to rest.

The setting sun felt good against his back and de Silva was looking forward to his visit to the de la Vegas. He felt certain things needed to be cleared up, mainly his harshness with Diego two weeks previously.

Bernardo admitted them to the *sala*, where Don Alejandro was sitting on the settee with his bandaged leg propped up. De Silva bowed. "Corporal Reyes told me what happened to you, Don Alejandro. I am sorry for the unfortunate incident."

"Mexico City has as much trouble selecting *comandantes* as Spain did," Alejandro said dryly.

"Someone in Mexico City is working behind the scenes to further his own vendetta," de Silva explained. "Villagro was apparently going to be paid well for killing Zorro. Hopefully, this action will end that possibility."

"How many of the soldiers are loyal to Villagro?" Alejandro asked pointedly. Bernardo brought in wine and poured a glassful for each man.

"I'll figure it out soon." De Silva sipped the wine. "Where is your son, Don Alejandro? I need to resolve something with him. I am afraid I said some harsh things to Diego the other day, and I wish to apologize."

"Yes, I assumed as much. Diego said to give his apologies, but he desired to avoid any further confrontations." Alejandro looked hard at the general.

"I will have to speak with him later, then." De Silva sighed. Suddenly, three armed men burst through the door, startling everyone inside.

"Diablo!" de Silva cried, reaching for his pistol. *Diablo's* shot grazed his arm, and the general dropped his pistol. Another man collected the remaining weapons. Corporal Reyes and Private Ortega seethed but made no move.

"Be grateful, General, that my aim was off. I seldom miss what I set out to shoot," *Diablo* smirked. "It is a shame that there are so many bandits in these hills that rob, plunder and kill. The whole *pueblo* will be talking about the crime at the de la Vega hacienda for some time to come, *señores*. Where is your son, de la Vega?"

"Out riding, Corporal," Alejandro retorted.

"I will station myself outside on the patio for a few minutes," Diablo said, "just in case de la Vega or Zorro shows up. Then, when I know we are alone, we will finish our business. Keep a close eye on this happy group, Rojas."

Diablo slipped out the door and onto the darkened patio.

Alejandro waited a minute and then on the pretense of shifting his injured leg, transferred the cane to his right hand and slammed it down on the arm of the soldier near him. The pistol went off with a booming noise, the bullet burying itself into the hardwood floor. In one swift move de Silva produced a small knife, which almost instantaneously buried itself in the chest of the other soldier. The private sank to the ground with a slight groan. The second soldier was quickly subdued.

An instant later, a reverberating shot echoed in the patio.

***

Zorro circled the hacienda and returned to the road from the pueblo. Even in the darkening sky, he could see that horses had passed by recently. Assuming them to be those of General de Silva and the *magistrado*, Zorro continued his circuit of the area, to come upon the *hacienda* away from the road.

Approaching the de la Vega home, the masked man noticed many horses, more than he felt feasible for the visit of just two officials and their escort. Riding Tornado near the outside wall, Zorro climbed to the top and slipped silently into the patio. A sudden shot from the *sala* turned his blood to ice, and he ran toward the main door.

A clicking noise made him turn around swiftly. A flash and a boom were the last things Zorro witnessed. He fell against the planter in the center of the patio.

Bernardo grabbed a pistol lying next to Rojas and ran to the *sala* window. Jerking away from the window, Bernardo signed what he had seen with his free hand. A man standing over a fallen body.

CHAPTER SIX

De Silva Takes Charge

"Zorro?" asked de Silva and Alejandro simultaneously. The *hacendado* grunted in pain as he heaved himself up from the settee.

"I will take care of *Diablo* and check on Bernardo's observations," de Silva said. "We must pray it is not Zorro, *señores*. Corporal Reyes, follow me."

The general opened the *sala* door a crack and then rushed out, hiding behind a pole that held up the balustrade. *Poor cover, but better than none*, he thought.

Reyes followed, hiding behind an adjacent one.

When de Silva's eyes adjusted to the lack of light, he could see nothing except the fallen man in the middle of the patio.

Rushing to the tree growing in the patio, de Silva crouched near Zorro; for he had determined it was the masked man. His heartbeat quickened at the thought. He motioning to Reyes, then whispered in his ear, "You stay with *Señor* Zorro and watch for any movement while I reconnoiter. Do not move him or touch him, Corporal."

"*Sí*, General," Reyes whispered back. After a short time, the general returned and lay down his pistol.

"*Diablo* has left. His horse is gone. Get Bernardo and light a several lanterns. I need to examine *Señor* Zorro's wound," he ordered. "And bring out Private Ortega. I may need his help as well."

With concern etched on his face, Alejandro hobbled behind Bernardo out to the patio. De Silva had removed the outlaw's hat and examined the grazing wound that the pistol ball had made just above Zorro's ear. It was difficult without taking off Zorro's mask, but the mask would remain until there were alone. The injury had bled profusely, but most of the bleeding had already stopped. The swollen area on the other side of Zorro's head caused de Silva concern. While not a doctor, he had some medical training under his belt, and battlefield experience, and the general knew head wounds were difficult.

Looking up, de Silva saw Reyes and Bernardo. They had followed his instructions, and the anxious face of Alejandro de la Vega looked over to him. "Is he alive?" came the husky whisper.

"*Sí*, Don Alejandro, he is. The ball grazed his head. But I think it is best that we find a comfortable place for him to stay until he regains consciousness," de Silva explained.

The old man's face clearly showed relief and he said, "Diego's room has a comfortable bed, and he won't mind."

"Reyes, Ortega, I want you to carry *Señor* Zorro up to Don Diego's room. He will rest there until he wakes up," the general said as he untied and slipped the cloak off the outlaw and handed it to Bernardo, along with the hat. Turning to the manservant, he said, while signing, "Bernardo, if you have a spring-house, I think it would be helpful if you brought a bucket of cool water, with clean linens. Zorro hit his head when he was shot, and a cool compress would be more effective than anything else." Bernardo nodded and went into the house.

Zorro was soon resting on Diego's bed, and Bernardo had brought in the desired items. De Silva ordered Corporal Reyes to take the prisoners into the *pueblo*, and posted Private Ortega outside of Diego's door. Then he reached for the mask. When he carefully lifted Zorro's head and untied the knot, Bernardo grabbed his wrist, shaking his head.

"Bernardo, I have known the identity of El Zorro since he saved me on the highway to Santa Barbara. Diego's secret is safe with me. Trust me."

Bernardo removed his hand and prepared the linen compresses. De Silva pulled off the blood-encrusted mask and laid it aside. The manservant handed him a compress and the general laid it against Diego's head. "Hold that there while I clean the wound." When he had finished, he sighed. Diego had not moved or made a sound during the entire procedure. I'll inform Don Alejandro about the situation. May I assume he is aware of Diego's double life?"

Bernardo nodded.

De Silva headed towards the door, then turned back with a slight smile. "Bernardo, I think Zorro may need a new mask. I suppose you can find one while I am gone. Diego will be fine for a few minutes." The general slipped out the door and closed it behind him. Reassuring the guard that the outlaw was still unconscious and under the watch of the de la Vega servant, de Silva walked down the stairs.

"Don Alejandro," de Silva said. "Zorro rests comfortably, with Bernardo attending him. I cannot tell you what his condition is until he wakes up. These injuries make it difficult to say, but I won't deceive you. However, I know this. If Zorro doesn't wake up soon and can't make an escape, they will take him to the pueblo. And as a representative of the Mexican government, I can do nothing to stop it. You must pray that *Señor* Zorro wakes up soon. I told Corporal Reyes not to rush to the *cuartel*, but he will have to report to Sergeant Garcia."

Alejandro nodded. "Thank you, General," he said. "I have grown fond of the outlaw in the past couple of years, and I can tell you I would not care for him to be captured, either."

"Zorro has been riding for two and a half years. Is that right, Don Alejandro?" de Silva asked, heading upstairs.

Alejandro nodded and then looked at him sharply. The general smiled and climbed the stairs to check on the injured man. He noted that a new mask lay next to young de la Vega, and the old one had disappeared.

Bernardo was applying a new compress to the wound and as he did so, Diego began moaning and moving around, making the manservant's job difficult. He mumbled something about an uncle.

***

Diego came out of a vault of darkness into a spinning, whirling world from his youth. His Uncle Esteban was spinning him on a rope, which the two had hung from a lofty, old oak tree. At first it had been fun, but as his uncle kept spinning him faster and faster, his joy turned to discomfort and then to misery. His head hurt and the world was an unkind thing, jumping crazily. "Uncle Esteban, stop, *por favor*. Stop, please."

But his uncle either did not hear him or didn't think he was serious. Finally, he had to let go.

And he woke up to a world still moving around like a storm-tossed ship, with Bernardo and de Silva gazing at him in concern. With a groan, he closed his eyes again to stop the unnatural motion. "Everything spinning, head hurts," he murmured. Diego felt his hands clenching the bed covers as though he could stop the motion by hanging on to something.

"Your head wound causes both dizziness and pain. Rest is best for you, but we lack that luxury. We need to figure out a way for you to escape," General de Silva explained.

Slowly, as the painF and dizziness receded a little, Diego opened his eyes again and looked carefully at the general, avoiding moving his head more than necessary. "What happened to me? The last thing I remember is riding in anticipation of your arrival here. I thought that maybe some of Villagro's soldiers might have tried to assassinate you, the *magistrado*, and Don Alejandro. Apparently, I was right. But I can remember almost nothing beyond that," Diego said in confusion.

"After taking us hostage, Corporal *Diablo* laid in wait for you. Your patron saint has been watching over you well, because *Diablo* is a very good shot."

"You are an officer in the Mexican Army, General de Silva. Why are you helping me?" he asked. "You have a duty to bring in outlaws."

"You are a patriot, *señor*, who has been branded an outlaw. I will never deliberately turn you in." De Silva smiled.

"General, did you pick Villagro for *comandante* of this *pueblo*? If so, you made a sorry choice."

"Look at the bright side. A Spanish lieutenant who came with me was being considered for the post. You could have been contending with José Rodriguez."

"That pompous fool? Heaven forbid," Diego retorted, and then realized what he had said. His eyes widened in shock. "You know." He reached up and felt for the mask, realizing it was gone.

"*Sí*, Diego, I have known since you saved us on the highway going to Santa Barbara. You may not have used the sword, but the footwork still gave you away. Do you think you could fool one who knows your every move?" de Silva asked softly. "Although your skills have sharpened since you left Spain. I knew you wouldn't be content sitting back and letting someone else handle a necessary task." De Silva's eyes gleamed with undisguised pride. "Now we need to get Zorro out of here and provide an alibi for you, Diego. You rest here quietly while I see if there is anything to ease the pain and dizziness. There's a guard at the door. I had no choice. We had to keep up pretenses, and that makes this difficult." He left, closing the door behind him.

Bernardo began signing to him. "Stop, Bernardo," Diego finally said after watching for a while. "Your fingers moving around like that are making me dizzier, and I think I know what you are saying. I wish it were as simple as going through the secret entrance. The problem lies in explaining my escape despite a head wound and a guarded door. It has to be something plausible if anyone was patrolling outside." He closed his eyes and pondered a moment, wishing the pain in his head would go away. When he heard the door latch click, he opened them again.

General de Silva had a mug of wine and a bottle of medicine. "This is the best I can do. It is a pain medicine, but it also makes one sleepy. I really dislike the idea of giving you a narcotic with your injury...."

"Then I should not take it," Diego interrupted de Silva. "The light-headedness is receding a bit, and the pain is tolerable. Considering the only solution, I do not need to be drugged."

"Over the balcony on your horse?" de Silva asked.

"*Sí*, general. That is the only other exit."

"Yes, if we can pull it off, then we can say that you overpowered me and made your escape. No one else knows, but us, the extent of your injury," de Silva thought out loud. "I assume your horse will stand still while you get down to him?"

"*Sí*, he will stand as long as I ask him to," Diego told him. Reaching over to the general, he tried to grab his arm, but seeing the blood on his sleeve, he stopped. "It would seem that you are injured as well, General."

"Just a flesh wound." Holding out with his other arm, de Silva let Diego grab it and pull himself up to a sitting position. Although the vertigo was almost overwhelming, the injured man stayed upright while Bernardo tied on the new mask. Soon, Zorro was trying to ease himself off the bed. Bernardo stood on one side to help steady him, and Zorro held on to de Silva's shoulder for balance.

De Silva motioned toward the balcony. "Bernardo, open up the balcony door. We'll receive some warning before the lancers arrive. And put out the candles. We show up too much on this open balcony. Oh, and Bernardo, I am most gratified at the speed with which your hearing has returned. I would almost say it was miraculous." The man-servant smiled sheepishly at the general as he carried out the instructions. Zorro chuckled at the servant's discomfiture.

"*Señor*, whistle for your horse," de Silva told Zorro. Making his way to the railing, the outlaw complied. As Tornado approached the window, Zorro peered down and felt like he was falling off a cliff. His stomach churned and he felt bile rising in his throat.

"I should not have done that," he murmured, gripping the railing tightly. At that moment, Sgt. Garcia's booming voice echoed from the hacienda's front entrance.

CHAPTER SEVEN

Zorro's Escape

"I believe I have thought of a way to give Diego an alibi, but I will need your help, Bernardo," the general said to the anxious servant.

"General, what is your plan?" Zorro asked quietly. The world continued to spin and dance.

"You will take the stallion to wherever you go when you are Zorro, and Bernardo will help you change into your regular clothes. He will lead you to the place where you will be located. The story will be that you were thrown from your horse, hitting your head on a rock," de Silva explained. "But you will have to remember that you were thrown from your horse and hit your head on a rock."

"I do not think I can do this, General," Zorro answered softly, trying desperately to gain control over his lack of equilibrium. It was extremely disconcerting, and he felt he was losing a battle over control of his own body. The pain in his head was like drums beating incessantly and the only thing keeping him up was the grip he had on the railing of the balcony, a grip so hard his fingers hurt.

"Zorro, you must do it," de Silva told him. "Can you climb down with your eyes closed? Then use your hands to guide you, and listen to my directions carefully."

Zorro took a deep breath in anticipation.

"Keep a tight grip on the railing and swing over it. Your horse is directly below you. Just slide down, use your hands to hold on until you feel the stallion's back under your feet," de Silva instructed him.

All the old training came into play. Zorro followed each direction explicitly as it was given and when he felt Tornado's back, he positioned himself and then let go of the railing, grabbing the horse's mane with both hands as soon as he had his seat.

"Tornado, the cave. Go to the cave, boy." Tornado trotted off in a circular path that would eventually take the pair to the secret cave.

***

As he watched Zorro ride away, de Silva breathed a sigh of relief, very much aware that this ordeal wasn't over yet. Turning to the increasingly anxious manservant, he gave the next set of instructions. "I want you to hit me with enough force to bring up a nice bruise. As soon as I make my excuses and leave, go to Diego. Follow the plan but be cautious with him. The injury is serious, and riding is harmful to him."

Bernardo cocked his fist back but couldn't quite get himself to throw the punch.

"Do it, Bernardo. To protect Diego, you must do it."

Bernardo threw a punch, sending the general to the floor. Looking up at the manservant, de Silva just smiled, felt his jaw, and then called out for help as Bernardo cowered by the fireplace.

"Zorro overpowered me!" de Silva called out.

Ortega burst through the door, wildly looking around the room. "Are you all right, General?"

Holding his hand to his jaw, de Silva nodded and pointed. "Zorro's injuries weren't as bad as I expected. He escaped over the balcony on his stallion. We must go after him!"

***

"Sí, General." The two men rushed out of the room, and Bernardo stood up. He shut the door and gathered Don Diego's clothes. Bernardo lit a lantern and dashed down the stone staircase. As he entered the main cave, he heard Tornado snorting. Zorro had already dismounted and was lying on a pile of hay.

Bernardo slid off the mask. "Just let me sleep, Bernardo. Leave me alone," Diego murmured, pushing the manservant's hand away. Despite his protests, Bernardo soon had Don Diego in his own clothes and ready to ride.

Diego, now more lucid, sat up and stared at the mute. "You are serious about me getting back up on a horse," he said. Bernardo nodded. Diego groaned. "You cannot imagine the nightmare that brief journey was on Tornado, and he is smooth gaited. Like a ship in a storm. In a hurricane," he added with a tight smile. Bernardo smiled back and shrugged.

Diego lay back down. "My head hurts terribly; all I want is sleep. If you have any intentions of getting me up on another horse, you had better do it soon. I really don't know how long I can stay awake." Bernardo signed his intention of getting a horse from the corral, asking Don Diego if he would be all right while he was away. Diego just gave a slight wave of his hand and rolled over on the hay

The mute frowned and left. Diego slipped into a sleep that Bernardo had difficulty waking him from when he returned a short while later. Shaking the caballero's arm, the manservant was almost in a panic when Diego finally woke up enough to blink groggily at him. "What am I doing here?"

Bernardo helped him up on a horse and then mounted behind him.

"I fell off my horse and hit my head. Is that what happened, Bernardo?" he asked, confused. Bernardo gave him a one-handed sign for yes, because he didn't know what else to tell him. "Where are we going?" was Diego's next question.

Of course, the manservant couldn't answer. His hands were occupied juggling the horse's reins and maintaining his patrón's balance, so the manservant couldn't answer. Reaching a well-traveled road not too far from the *hacienda*, Bernardo dismounted and helped the injured man down from the horse. Don Diego was unconscious almost before he was off the horse. Worried, Bernardo, nevertheless, mounted and rode back to the *hacienda*, entering the house as unobtrusively as he could. He gave a signal to Don Alejandro.

"Zorro may have been grazed by that pistol ball, but he was not injured so much that he could not give me this as he escaped," de Silva emphasized, rubbing his jaw as he spoke to Sgt. Garcia. The bruise was coloring nicely, Bernardo noted.

"Yes, that rascal of a Zorro always seems to escape, even when it does not seem possible for him to do so," Garcia commented sagely.

Walking up to Don Alejandro, Bernardo tapped him on the shoulder to get his attention, then he started signing that Don Diego's horse had come back to the *hacienda* without him. "Diego's horse came back riderless?" Alejandro asked in confirmation, his voice rising in fatherly concern. Bernardo nodded.

"He might have been thrown," Sgt. Garcia conjectured, a worried frown on his face. "Corporal *Diablo* is also out there somewhere."

"Sergeant Garcia, we must go out and look for young de la Vega," de Silva said. The general and lancers left the hacienda, following Bernardo's directions. A waxing moon had risen and aided the searchers.

It was only a short time later that Sgt. Garcia discovered Diego, lying motionless by the side of a dusty road. As he gently turned the injured man over, Diego opened his eyes and gave Garcia a puzzled look.

"Thrown … horse … my head … so tired …"

Then he lost consciousness again in the sergeant's arms.

"It is all right, Don Diego, we will get you home." Garcia held him as a lancer approached with a lantern. "Corporal Reyes, fire your musket. That will inform the others that we have found Don Diego. And then send someone to the *hacienda* to bring a carriage. It's best if he avoids riding a horse." Everyone speedily complied with Garcia's orders as he gazed uneasily at his injured friend.

A short time later, Diego was at home and under the care of General de Silva. After checking the gunshot wound and applying a bandage, the general and Bernardo, took turns throughout the night watching over Diego. Alejandro sat awake in the *sala*, praying. During the early morning hours, Alejandro laboriously made his way up the stairs and took his turn at his son's bedside. Throughout the entire day, Diego remained unconscious. The young man stirred from sleep as midnight approached.

A small candle illuminated the room. Bernardo was sleeping by the bedside in a chair, and Diego looked at him, wondering what had happened, that he was lying in his own bed with a bandage wrapped around his head. Touching one side of his head, he found the answer for the bandage, but couldn't recall how it happened. As he lay on the bed, jumbled memories bounced around in his head. He fell asleep trying to make sense of them all.

The next time he awoke, it was to the smell of steaming coffee. His father was reclining in the chair, sipping his coffee. Another cup sat on the bedstand, and Diego concluded someone must have just brought it in. Seeing his father's bandaged leg, some of his past reordered itself in coherent patterns.

Looking up, Alejandro saw Diego gazing at him with a slight frown on his face. "Diego, my son, you have finally awakened. How do you feel?" he asked, the relief evident in his voice.

"Confused. I feel like I've missed something, especially the reason for the bandage on my head. I keep thinking of being thrown off a horse, but I also keep seeing images of a pistol going off in the dark." Diego reached for the coffee and sipped it as he waited for his father to explain things.

When Alejandro had completed the account, Diego was astonished. "Have I really been asleep for more than a day? And General de Silva knows about Zorro? I wish I could remember more." He shook his head and winced at a momentary sharp pain.

A short time later, the general arrived at the *hacienda*, inquiring into the wellbeing of young de la Vega. He beamed as he came into Diego's room. "I am happy you are recovering so well, Diego, my boy. You really had me worried."

Diego just smiled. He sat up, his back was stiff and sore.

"Any lingering pain or dizziness?" de Silva asked.

"Just a little pain," Diego answered. "General, who gave you that illustrious shiner on your cheek?"

"Bernardo did," de Silva laughed. "The cover-up required skill, but not to that extent."

Diego laughed along with his teacher. Bantering like this again felt good. It reminded him of the days in Spain, with the only thing missing being Fernando. He sighed, "You know, General, I really hated having to deceive you the way I did."

"And I am sorry for the way I treated you, Diego. Whether you had given up your military skills or not, I should not have been so harsh."

"I suppose that one act deserved the other, but it is over."

"You need never fear that I will compromise your position either, Diego. This wasn't what I had in mind for a leadership role, but I'm even prouder of this accomplishment than if you had led a battalion. Your role has taken great courage and sacrifice." De Silva's eyes shone with pride. He noticed the same light in Alejandro's eyes.

Diego felt self-conscious. "It was only what was necessary, but it escalated into more than I planned."

A knock interrupted the conversation. Diego said, "Enter." Garcia appeared to highly agitated. "Many pardons, General, Don Diego. Oh, I am so glad to see you feeling better," he told Diego, then remembered his errand. "General, the *magistrado* has been kidnapped."

"Again?"

CHAPTER EIGHT

Decisions

D*iablo* left the scene of chaos and slipped out through the stable area and out of the hacienda where the horses waited. "I have finished here. Zorro will never bother me again," he growled as he mounted. "Let's get back to the pueblo and report to the *comandante*." He swung on his prancing mount. Jerking the reins enough for the horse to squeal, it nevertheless stood still.

"The comandante has been stripped of his command. What can we do?" Private Braza asked. His eyes were large in the shadows. "How do we claim the reward for Zorro?"

"We don't right now. We can effect the comandante's release and then he will tell us the next steps." *Diablo* hoped Capitan Villagro would have a plan. "Come."

The two men rode toward the pueblo at a full gallop. As they reached the outskirts, they slowed, walking their mounts to the cuartel.

The outer gate was locked, but the guard opened for them and accompanied them to the stables. "Do you want me to take care of the horses?" Private Diaz asked.

"You are on duty," *Diablo* snapped. "Braza will do that. You accompany me to the comandante's office."

"The comandante is under house arrest," the soldier pointed out.

"I know that, Private! I still want to see him."

"*Si*, Corporal." Private Diaz pulled out his key and put it in the door.

Diablo moved closer behind the soldier.

As they passed into the stygian blackness of the outer office, *Diablo* pulled out his knife and plunged it into the private's back. Diaz slid to the ground with a soft exhale of air.

Diablo looked down at the body lying at his feet.

The dead soldier looked peaceful in death, more than the magistrado and his friends would be, when he had the chance to exact his revenge on them. Taking the keys from the dead guard, the corporal unlocked the door and stepped in.

"Capitán, I have come to free you, so we can rightfully take back that which is ours."

Silence.

"*Capitán*," *Diablo* said a little louder.

Villagro must be sleeping, he thought. What can we do after we escape? Will Villagro want to become an outlaw? No, but Zorro is dead and I can kill de Silva and the magistrado, then Villagro could report to his superior in Mexico City. Without the general and Magistrado Hernandez, it would be Villagro's word against anyone else's. Yes, that would work.

Diablo studied the form on the bed.

"This is not the time to sleep," *Diablo* muttered. "*Capitán!* Wake up! Only a short while before the dawn! Capitán!"

Striding over to the bed, he saw in the dim light the slumbering form of the former comandante. Disgusted his leader would sleep when so much needed to be done, he reached over and shook Villagro, and then jerked his hand back, a quick burst of fear exploding in his gut. The sleeping form was unnaturally stiff. Gaining his composure, *Diablo* reached over again and pulled the blanket off the bed. And found a corpse.

Cursing, *Diablo* lit a candle stub on the nightstand and studied the body. No evidence he had been shot, but there was a puddle of blood on the floor. Then the corporal checked Villagro's wrists and found them slashed. A knife lay next to the capitán's stomach. Suicide? The soldier felt a shiver course down his spine. *Diablo* realized this changed everything. With Villagro dead, that left him with nothing. Villagro was a weaker man than he had thought.

With Villagro's suicide, *Diablo* realized he was left to take the brunt of Mexican justice. If Villagro had remained alive, his rank and leadership abilities, with promises of promotion and power, could have enticed more men. Especially if de Silva and Hernandez were dead. No one would follow *Diablo* now. In disgust, he threw the blanket back over the dead man, dragged the dead soldier into the same room, and then left, locking the door behind him. *Diablo* didn't doubt that his two compatriots at the de la Vega hacienda would blame him for everything.

Rushing out of the cuartel, *Diablo* threw the keys into the well and, taking a lancer's horse, mounted and rode out of the pueblo. Braza gazed at him, waiting for him to give orders. *Diablo* didn't want baggage. Even though Braza followed directions and had a mean streak, he didn't know how loyal the private would be. *Diablo* had to think, be alone. Figure things out.

As he rode away, a sudden thought occurred to him. Now that he was a wanted criminal, he should embrace his fate and destroy as many enemies as possible in his new career. At least he would not have to worry about Zorro interfering with his activities. The Fox was dead. Laughing, *Diablo* continued down the road, pondering which of his two enemies he would destroy first.

That night, after making a rudimentary camp, *Diablo* stared into a small fire. Hernandez was the logical choice. Señor Hernandez, the old magistrado, had complained of fatigue much of the time since returning from Santa Barbara and would be much easier to abduct. If he could abduct the magistrado, then he could set up a perfect trap for de Silva. A ransom, too. Then he could ride north and gather loyal men.

The fire flickered off the rocks. These hills were a perfect place for an ambush. He chuckled. *Diablo* would do much better as a brigand than working for the Mexican government. Much better.

The flames from the campfire made orange shadows across his hands. His echoing laugh seemed to come from the depths of hell. It would be perfect. With that happy thought, *Diablo* curled up in his blanket and drifted off into a sound sleep.

The next morning, *Diablo* set out to implement his plans. After he had stolen peon's clothing, and changed, he rode bareback into the pueblo, not noticed by anybody. After all, who noticed lowly peons. Entering the tavern, he held a package in his arms and approached the innkeeper. "Señor, I have a package I was ordered to give to the magistrado," he said, keeping his head bowed and his manner subservient.

"Who sent it?" the innkeeper asked moving closer.

Diablo took a step back, head still bowed. "From General de Silva. I was sent by him and Don Alejandro."

"What is it?"

Diablo shook his head slightly. "They didn't tell me, but I got the idea that it was the Magistrado Hernandez's bottles of medicine." From just under the brim of the beat up straw hat, *Diablo* saw the innkeeper rubbing his chin. "They sent me because the deaf/mute was taking care of Don Diego." *Diablo* had heard the gossip as he was preparing for his little adventure.

"Don Diego?"

"Si, he was hurt on the *rancho*."

"Not badly, I hope."

"I do not know, *señor*."

"Upstairs, the room on the far end," the innkeeper told him.

Diablo climbed up the stairs, a smile playing about his lips. He pulled out an envelope from inside his shirt and left the package with the 'medicine' on a chair. Then he knocked.

"Enter."

Diablo opened the door and slipped inside. Hernandez was standing at the balcony, in his fancy magistrado's uniform, gazing out into the tavern's inner courtyard. He turned enough to gaze at the peon. "What is it?"

"A letter from General de Silva."

"Hand it here."

Diablo bowed and handed the letter over to the old man.

With a frown, Hernandez tore open the envelope and read the note.

Diablo wasn't familiar with de Silva's handwriting, but he was with Capitán Villagro's fancy script and had copied that.

Hernandez's frown deepened. "This doesn't look like the general's handwriting."

Diablo stood right in front of Hernandez, the point of his knife caressing the magistrado's Adam's apple. "You will not cry out. You will do everything I tell you and when I tell you."

"Who are you? What is this?" Hernandez sputtered.

Diablo jerked off the straw hat and tossed it behind him. "Think about it, Magistrado. Regardless, this is a kidnapping for ransom and you are the victim." *Diablo* pointed to the bed. "Sit down." He grabbed the cord holding the curtain at the balcony. Then he trussed up Hernandez so that he could barely move. Finally, he stuffed a handkerchief into the magistrado's mouth and tied the ends around the back of his head tight.

"We are going to wait for a while, then we will leave quietly." *Diablo* cracked the door and peered out onto the balcony overlooking the main room of the tavern. There were very few patrons this time of the morning. He grabbed the package and shut and locked the door. Hernandez stared at him with frightened eyes, and *Diablo* tore open the box. The bottle sat in pristine glory, waiting for him to make use of it. Wrapped around it was a uniform.

An hour later, a knock made *Diablo* jump. He went to the door and cracked it. Making his voice slightly higher, he imitated the nasal tone of the magistrado. "What do you want?"

"It's your breakfast, Magistrado." It was the barmaid.

"Set it on the chair and I'll get it when I finish getting dressed."

"Sí, señor." Her light steps faded down the stairs.

Finally, he reached his arm out and pulled in the tray. While the magistrado moaned on the bed, *Diablo* finished a wonderfully filling breakfast. He did the same with the tray of food sent up at lunch.

Then the corporal loosened Hernandez's gag and made him take some of the 'medicine' in the bottle. While it took effect, *Diablo* changed into the uniform, minus any decorations. He pulled a pair of Hernandez's boots from the wardrobe and tried them on. A little tight, but they would do. *Diablo* jerked Hernandez to his feet and untied his hands. The magistrado wavered as though he was going to fall, but *Diablo* held him steady. "You will do exactly as I say. You will walk out of the room. I will be on your right side. We will walk down the steps, slowly, but steadily. You will say nothing, or my knife will find itself a new home in your back. We will walk through the back of the tavern and to the stable where we will take your carriage and drive out of the pueblo. Do you understand, Magistrado?"

Hernandez nodded, his eyes slightly unfocused.

Diablo checked outside the door, waiting until the tavern was empty. "Come, Señor Magistrado. Remember, my knife is ready to end your life right now, but if you cooperate, then you have a chance to live."

Slowly, the pair walked to the top of the stairs. There *Diablo* stopped. "One step at a time," he murmured. Down they went, *Diablo* holding on to the magistrado's arm. They reached the bottom, and *Diablo* guided the older man toward the back door, the one leading out to the stable.

The innkeeper walked out of the kitchen and gave the pair a questioning look.

"The magistrado wanted to get some fresh air. We are taking the carriage." *Diablo* didn't stop.

"Very good, señor. I will have Ramon harness the horse," the inkeeper said as they were exiting.

"Gracias," *Diablo* said over his shoulder. When they reached the carriage, he helped Hernandez into the carriage and joined him. The boy soon had the horse hitched to the carriage, and *Diablo* wasted no time getting out of the pueblo. He drove to the same secluded area he had slept in the night before. After tying up the old man again and leaving him in the carriage, *Diablo* pulled out some writing materials he had found in the magistrado's room. Then he composed a very terse but to the point letter. It would be delivered the next morning and by the end of the day, the trap would be sprung and the former corporal would be a great deal richer.

***

De Silva knew he should visit the magistrado but was concerned about Diego. When Alejandro offered him the guest room, the general accepted. He rode into the pueblo late the morning after Diego's injury in order to take the two treasonous soldiers to the cuartel and to check on Villagro. A note from Garcia told him that a scuffle had occurred in the outer office, one of the guards was missing, and Villagro wasn't answering his door. With a sigh, the general tugged on the rope attached to the lancers' horses. One lay across the saddle, dead, and the other sat tied and gagged. He had already heard enough about *Diablo's* involvement in the plot to kill Zorro, and Villagro's involvement in everything about Zorro to causing chaos in the local government. He wasn't sure what was true and what was just a soldier trying to make excuses for his involvement.

The general wondered just what Garcia did when he was the person in charge. Of course, with Zorro around, Garcia's leadership stood on firmer ground. De Silva rode into the cuartel and handed the rope to one of the guards at the gate. "Put this man in a cell for court martial later this week. Then take the dead man to be buried." He dismounted and strode to the comandante's quarters. Garcia met him. "Have you gone into the capitán's office yet?"

With a salute, Garcia declared, "No, General. Uh, I wanted to…"

"Nevermind. Let's check now. You said there was a soldier missing?"

"Sí, General. Actually two. Private Diaz. He had guard duty last night. And Private Brazas is also missing along with a horse."

Nodding, de Silva opened the outer door and let the sunlight show him a puddle of dried blood on the floor. "Do you have the key to the inner room?"

Garcia stepped around the puddle of blood. "Sí, General. I have the master set."

"Then open the door."

"But General, maybe the capitán is, uh, in his altogether."

"He would have said so, Sergeant. Open the door."

Garcia unlocked the door and pushed it open. A sliver of light coming from the bedroom window broke the darkness.

De Silva noticed the body of Private Diaz just inside the door. He saw the mound on the bed. He was pretty sure what had happened. There were the beginnings of the smell of death. He checked the corpses and let the blanket cover Villagro's body again. After examining Diaz's body, he pulled another blanket from the bed and covered the private's body. "Prepare Diaz for a proper military funeral. Have someone contact the priest and the undertaker to make arrangements. I will let the magistrado know of these events."

He turned away.

"What about the capitán?"

"Have him buried soon. No military funeral." De Silva strode across the plaza and entered the tavern. It was empty.

The innkeeper approached. "Are you here for refreshment, General?"

"No. I was going to visit the magistrado."

"You just missed him. He wanted some fresh air and left in his carriage."

De Silva scratched under his chin then he rubbed his eyes. During siesta? He nodded and left. Perhaps he would see him near the pueblo. After the arrangements for the dead men had been made, the general headed back out to the de la Vega hacienda. He had not seen the magistrado, but he would see him in the morning. A bed would feel particularly wonderful this night. Hopefully, Diego should be better. He was a strong young man.

***

A knock crashed in on Sergeant Garcia's dreams. And they were such pleasant dreams. Three women were fawning over him, wanting to hear of his exploits chasing Zorro. Another one served him wine. The pounding continued along with Corporal Reyes' muffled voice calling his name. Garcia opened his eyes to his own little room. No women, no wine.

"Sergeant Garcia! Wake up!"

"I am awake, *baboso*," Garcia grumbled. He pushed himself out of bed and stumbled to his door. The sun was just peeking through his window. What could be happening this time of the day? Garcia cracked his door open just as Reyes started knocking again.

The door banged against Garcia and Reyes shoved a piece of paper under the sergeant's nose. "Sergeant, the *magistrado* has been kidnapped."

"What?" Garcia opened the door all the way, and grabbed the paper. He read it slowly out loud. "Bring ten thousand *pesos* to Rancho La Brea by the middle of the afternoon or the magistrado will be killed. Do not come before." Garcia's eyes widened in shock.

"Sí, Sergeant and ten thousand pesos is a lot of money."

"Sundown," Garcia murmured. Then he folded the paper and thrust it back into Reyes' hands. He scratched his stubbly cheek. "Let me get dressed, then we will go looking for Magistrado Hernandez."

"But the note said not to come before sundown, Sergeant. And come with ten thousand pesos. How are we going to get ten thousand pesos?"

"I will go out to the de la Vega hacienda and give the ransom note to General de Silva. You take a few of the men and try to get ten thousand pesos."

"Who do we ask?"

"The rancheros, the merchants, anybody."

"Sí, Sergeant." He turned away from the door.

"Baboso! Give me the note. I have to show it to General de Silva."

After handing it back, Reyes clattered down the stairs and shouted to several of the men.

Garcia pulled on his uniform, splashed water on his face and tucked the letter into his pocket. Then he strode to the stable, where one of the men was saddling his horse. Reyes tapped his foot impatiently.

"What are you waiting for?"

"Sergeant, didn't Capitán Villagro have a chest with all the fines he collected?"

Garcia opened his mouth and shut it again. "He did. Do you think it had ten thousand pesos in it?"

"It wouldn't hurt to find out," Reyes said.

"No, and we would have the ransom ready by this afternoon."

The two men walked to the office, which Garcia still thought reeked of death and blood. He made the sign of the cross. Reyes copied him. In the corner of the office stood the comandante's chest. It was locked. None of Garcia's keys fit, but Reyes pulled out his pistol and shot at the lock. It only knicked it.

"Go get a shovel and a pick," Garcia said. "We'll get into it somehow."

The trunk finally caved into their combined efforts and Garcia saw various bags of coins as well as loose currency. "Count it to see if there is enough for the ransom. I am going to take this to the general."

Although he wanted breakfast first, there was no time for that. So much happened yesterday and now more was happening today. The guard opened the gate and Garcia's horse lumbered through the plaza and out of the pueblo. Dust roiled under the big gelding's feet and sweat rolled down Garcia's face before he was halfway to the hacienda.

One of the de la Vega servants met him at the gate and watched his horse. Garcia hustled into the patio area and then up the steps to Don Diego's room, where he had been told the general was. Garcia would be able to see how Don Diego was doing.

***

De Silva paled as he read the note.

"When, Sergeant?"

"This morning, probably not more than two hours ago, General. I have already ordered lancers out to comb the hills."

"Good, I will accompany you back to the cuartel," de Silva informed Garcia. "Diego, I'll return to visit once I've located the magistrado. *Adios*." He rushed out, a worried frown on his face.

Diego had remained silent during this entire conversation and now stared at the door through which his teacher had left.

"Diego, I know your look. Let the general deal with this. Your injury has not healed completely," Alejandro admonished his son. Diego nodded and continued to drink his coffee.

Soon, Alejandro got up and stretched. "Now you are awake and seemingly on the road to recovery, I am going to change into some clean clothes and freshen up a bit. I'm very glad you are better. I was extremely worried about you."

"Gracias, Father. Take all the time you need. In fact, you look tired. Perhaps a nap would help."

Alejandro smiled, then limped out. Once his father had left, Diego slipped out of bed. A bit unsteady, he nevertheless felt well enough to do what was necessary. He had almost finished changing in the secret room when the soft whooshing noise of the secret panel alerted him to someone's entrance. Looking up, he saw his father's eyes boring into his own.

"Diego, is it really necessary for you to do this so soon after having been shot?" he asked plaintively.

"Sí, Father, I believe so. It seems *Diablo* is involved. We are aware of his ruthlessness. I can also guess the reason for the kidnapping of the magistrado is to force the general to come where the corporal can kill him, thus effecting the revenge of the two men he most hates."

Diego smiled as he tied the mask on. "I hope surprise will balance the scales in favor of General de Silva, since *Diablo* probably thinks I'm dead." He winced slightly while adjusting the bandanna and donning the hat. "Father, do not worry. This time I will not rush stupidly into an ambush." He smiled and started down the stone steps, leaving his father alone in the little room.

"Be careful, Diego," Alejandro said to the empty stairs.

Zorro prepared Tornado for the ride. He felt lightheaded and somewhat lethargic, but believed this would pass. As he bent down to pull up the cinch, Bernardo grabbed the strap and motioned him out of the way. Straightening up, Zorro nodded. Sometimes, he felt Bernardo must be able to read his mind.

"Gracias, Bernardo," Zorro said. "The cinch was a little difficult."

Bernardo signed a query as to the wisdom of Zorro's venture.

Sighing, Zorro gave the same explanation he gave to his father. "I cannot just lay in bed and hope all goes well. I respect and admire the general too much."

Bernardo smiled and signed a statement about Zorro's commitment as well.

Zorro laughed and shrugged. "I suppose so. Zorro won't stop wearing the mask until all men have good hearts."

Mounting, he rode Tornado out of the cave and into the bright morning sunlight. The bright light burned into his eyes, causing a slight renewal of the former pain. After a few moments, he kicked the stallion into a rolling canter toward the pueblo.

Audaciously riding through the cuartel gates to save time, Zorro shouted for Sgt. Garcia or General de Silva. Instead, he got Corporal Reyes.

"Señor Zorro!" Reyes said in shock.

"Where is General de Silva?" Zorro demanded.

"He and Sgt. Garcia are delivering ransom for the *magistrado.*"

"If you value the lives of the general, Sergeant Garcia, and the *magistrado,* tell me the direction General de Silva went to find *Diablo.*" Zorro wasn't in the mood to banter, and he ignored the small group of lancers gathering.

"He received a note saying Rancho La Brea, and bring two-thousand pesos. The general assumed that was the spot where an exchange would be made," Reyes explained. "They finally gathered the pesos together just in the last half hour."

"*Gracias*, Corporal. And I believe the General and Sergeant Garcia are walking into an ambush." At Zorro's command, Tornado spun around and galloped out the still open gates.

Reyes pondered the last statement for half a minute and then acted. "Lancers, to horse! We must warn Sergeant Garcia!"

Zorro knew he had to urge Tornado to gallop even faster if he wanted to reach the Rancho La Brea before *Diablo* killed da Silva and the magistrado. Guiding Tornado off the regular road, Zorro took a narrow path dangerous at this pace. "Be sure of foot, Tornado," he admonished the horse, leaning over his steed's neck. The pace and rough path were hard on both of them, but Zorro didn't slow the stallion down.

The end of the path came out of the hills just above the La Brea Tar Pits and near the entrance of the rancho. As he crested the hill, Zorro finally pulled Tornado to a stop and reconnoitered the area. To his right, about halfway down the hill, he saw a slight movement. On more careful perusal, the movement revealed *Diablo* in hiding.

The *magistrado* was bound, gagged, and laying to one side, while *Diablo* watched the trail.

Soon, the general's small group rode into view. The general dismounted and started for the signpost near the tar pits. As de Silva came within ten feet of his destination, *Diablo* rose for his shot at the *magistrado*.

Zorro brought Tornado upright rearing on his hind legs, the stallion's screaming challenge echoing among the hills.

Diablo pivoted around, blanching at the sight of the masked man.

"You are dead!" he shouted, aiming his rifle. As *Diablo's* finger squeezed the trigger, the magistrado kicked the corporal's feet, putting Diablo off balance. The shot whistled well above Tornado's head.

Laughing, Zorro urged Tornado into a run down the hillside. Reaching *Diablo* before the corporal regained his footing, Zorro grabbed the devil by the collar, hoisted him up and threw him over the saddle. Zorro's head pounded again, but he ignored it. He had accomplished his aim of thwarting *Diablo's* planned ambush.

"Magistrado, thank you for your help. I must deliver the prisoner and then I will return to untie you." The magistrado nodded behind his gag.

Tornado made his way down to the waiting group who had come with the money, and Zorro dumped *Diablo* to the ground. The corporal tried to jump up and run, but de Silva's blade at his Adam's apple stopped him.

"Again, Señor Zorro, you have saved me at the risk of your own life. My thanks to you, *Dominar*," de Silva said with feeling.

Zorro blinked in surprise. De Silva refered to his as *dominant master*, a term of great honor.

"*Gracias*, General," he said. "I cannot stay. I must return to *Señor* Hernandez. *Adios, señores.*"

A salute and he was riding back up the hill.

When he reached the magistrado, he gingerly dismounted and, kneeling, untied the kidnapped man. "Magistrado, can you walk down the hill unaided? More lancers are coming, and I must ride."

"Sí, *Señor* Zorro. I am grateful for your intervention yet again." The magistrado began walking toward the soldiers below.

Zorro watched for a moment before mounting and riding back home. By the time he reached the secret cave, he was more than ready to follow the admonition his father had given him earlier in the day. Bernardo was waiting and motioned for him to leave the horse and get back to bed. Zorro complied meekly.

When he awoke near sundown, General Juan de Silva's frowning face greeted him. "What is the matter with you, riding out this morning, you young idiot? How does your head feel?"

Diego grinned in return. "Much better for my nap, General. And no, I have no further plans for riding soon."

"Diego, do you remember when I said I was surprised you hadn't married yet? Your father told me what happened in Monterey a year and a half ago when you wanted to marry the young señorita. He feels guilty for his role in thwarting your happiness."

"I know he does," Diego said.

He explained in greater detail how his father cornered him in the stable sometime back. Diego had decided to reveal to everyone his dual identity and claim amnesty. Alejandro discouraged him, explaining Zorro was still needed in th *pueblo*. At that moment Diego had pictured Anna Maria in his mind and remembered the last kiss he had given her as Zorro before he left her. He realized later she had been enamored with 'Zorro,' and had no interest in Diego. It was a dilemma that frustrated him. The pain of the event with Anna Maria had receded, but never gone away.

"I understand now the necessity of it, and I am grateful to him," he told daSilva. "If I marry, I can't ride as Zorro. As long as I ride as Zorro, I cannot marry. I can't risk more loved ones being in danger."

"I don't believe that, Diego. I will tell you what I told your father. Do you remember me telling you a little about my beloved wife, who passed into the hereafter before I started teaching in Madrid?"

Diego nodded.

"She and I married when I was a young lieutenant rising in the ranks. Her father told her the life of a soldier's wife was fraught with heartache and anxiety. Unlike many fathers, though, he would not forbid her to marry me."

De Silva walked to the balcony as he continued his story. "Rosa's father was correct. I was absent during Miguel's birth and engaged in war against England when Elesa was a mere infant. I came home when my daughter turned two. I had sent three letters the whole time. Do you know what greeted me when I came home?"

Diego shook his head. Was the general was trying to discourage him or cheer him up? If it was the latter, de Silva wasn't succeeding.

"I found a pile of candle stubs in the flower bed under the sala window. There were six hundred and forty, to be exact. When I asked about it her comment was she lit a candle for me every day I was gone, with faith I would return. Despite the fear in her eyes, she never pleaded for me to back out of the assignment. She showed her love fiercely when I was home, and I felt her support when I was gone.

"My point, Diego, is to find someone similar and let her help you in your quest for justice. Many women can strengthen you during tough times. You cannot continue being this hero all alone. And, of course, you must have the pleasure of raising sons and daughters."

Diego said nothing. Who could know what lay ahead for him? But for some reason now, it seemed brighter and much less lonely.

SUSAN KITE

Author

S usan Kite has been writing for over thirty years, beginning with fan-fiction. A visit to the Mission San Luis Rey in 2001 became the catalyst to write her first novel, *My House of Dreams*. She now has over thirteen books published in various genres. Science fiction, fantasy, tall tales, and historical fiction for children, middle grades readers, young adults, and adults. Bold Venture Press published her trilogy *Zorro's Pacific Odyssey* — which consists of *The Outward Journey*, *The Forbidden Country*, and *The Deadly Homecoming* — and several of her Zorro short stories.

The author worked in school libraries for 35 years, mostly elementary and mostly in Tennessee. Reading has always been an important hobby for her. Now retired, Ms. Kite lives in Yukon, Oklahoma, with two opinionated black cats and a Jack Russell terrier.

PEREGO

Illustrator

S ingle named artist, Perego, has been creating art professionally for decades. His art and murals have won various awards, in the advertising industry, as well as both city and national awards.

He was recently honored with the most prestigious award given in the United States, the Presidential Lifetime Achievement Award. The award that recognizes individuals who have dedicated a significant portion of their lives to volunteer service. It's the highest award given to a U.S. citizen.

Perego's artwork is described as forceful, emotional and intuitive, powerful and passionate, exciting and magnetic. Gifted with an artistic family legacy hailing from the small Province of Perego, in northern Italy, he immediately showed talent in art, theater and music and seemed destined for creativity at an early age.

Perego grew up in the areas of New York, Pennsylvania and New Jersey. He briefly attended The Joe Kubert School of Cartoon and Graphic Art, where he studied under the Disney legend Milt Neil, before embarking on a freelance career including airbrush, portraiture and large scale murals. In the early 1990s he relocated to central Florida where he began applying his talents to interior design to public spaces, including night clubs, coffeehouses, restaurants, & surf shops. He's worked as an Art Director for industry giants, including Disney, Universal Studios, BET, Univision, and PBS to name a few. Now the Senior Art Director for *Lost Worlds*, he designs themed entertainment centers around the country.

Perego has illustrated many books, including cover paintings and black & white illustrations for Bold Venture Press. His work helped bring attention to the award-winning story "Death of a Grandee" by John French in *Zorro: The Daring Escapades*. He has illustrated stories in *Zorro's Exploits*, and *Zorro: Swordplay and Romance*.

Perego's major lifetime achievement is the founding of the international organization called the Art Army. This global family of artists is in more than 120 cities across the planet & has created a movement in itself. They believe that, "Everyone is an an artist, that we are all are creative, and that we all have a Creator Spark within us."

Learn more at www.Artofperego.com and www.ArtArmy.org

(1) My backdrop for Stevie Wonder's concert at World of Sports at Walt Disney World. (2) This mural won the National Downtown Redevelopment Award for Pioneer Park in Deland, Florida. (3) The parking garage for Daytona Lagoon. (4) I painted this for Disney's 25th anniversary.

BILL COTTER

Introduction

Bill Cotter has had a long-time fascination with Disney television. One of his earliest childhood memories is watching the Mickey Mouse Club with a younger brother, saying it was probably one of the few times they were so quiet together. Around that time, Disney introduced the ZORRO television series starring Guy Williams in the duel roles of Don Diego de la Vega, the son of a wealthy landowner in Spanish California, and as his alter ego, Zorro, who rode to fight injustice and oppression. It aired on ABC, Thursdays at 8:00 P.M. during 1957-58 and 1958-59 seasons.

Like many other children of the 50s, he was captivated by the series, both for the stories and Guy's portrayal of the masked avenger.

Years of watching the weekly anthology series eventually led to his working at the studio in Burbank, where he met his wife on a soundstage. He worked also at Disneyland, Walt Disney World, and WED (now Imagineering.)

During his time at Disney he co-founded an employee's club to showcase the company's old television shows, ostensibly to educate others on this aspect of Disney history. In actuality, the club was a vehicle for him to see the old programs.

Bill later left for another film studio, but his ongoing research into Disney's television history made him a semi-permanent resident of the Disney Archives, culminating in his 1997 book *The Wonderful World of Disney Television*.

He also was a key contributor to the "40 Years of Disney Television Magic" special which aired in 1994.

Bill has been featured on several Disney DVDs and documentaries, including several episodes of the Disney+ series *Behind the Attraction*. He has shared his love of Disney television at numerous fan conventions, including two D23 events.

In his spare time, he has written thirteen books on world's fairs, was named the Volunteer of the Year for the Los Angeles PD, and keeps busy with the Boy Scouts, where he was selected to the Eagle Scout Hall of Fame.

His extensive look at Walt Disney's version of *Zorro* can be found at https://www.billcotter.com/zorro/index.htm. There he shares memories of some by-gone times, a wealth of Disney information, and a look at some of his favorite things., including information on the books he has written and some other projects he's done over the years.

The Wonderful World of Disney Television (Disney Editions, 1997) is the culmination of Bill's ongoing research into Disney's television history.

JOHNSTON McCULLEY

Creator of Zorro

Zorro's name and likeness have been known world-wide, ever since the character's debut in *The All-Story Weekly*, a popular weekly magazine. Zorro sprang from the busy typewriter of Johnston McCulley (1883-1958). Born in Ottowa, Illinois, and raised in the neighboring town of Chillicothe, he began his writing career as a police reporter.

He contributed to popular magazines of the day like *Argosy*, *Western Story Magazine*, *Detective Story Magazine*, and *Blue Book*. Eventually he turned to writing film and television screenplays.

Inspired by the success of Zorro, McCulley developed several feature-length novels set in Spanish California. Magazines like *Argosy* often touted them as stories from "Zorro-land!" His other characters were The Crimson Clown, Thubway Tham, The Thunderbolt, and The Green Ghost.

McCulley died in 1958 in Los Angeles, California.

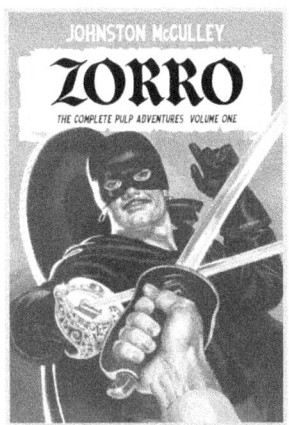

ZORRO ®

The Complete Pulp Adventures by Johnston McCulley

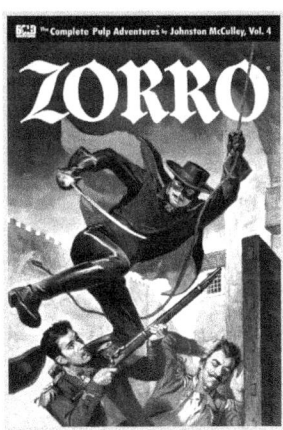

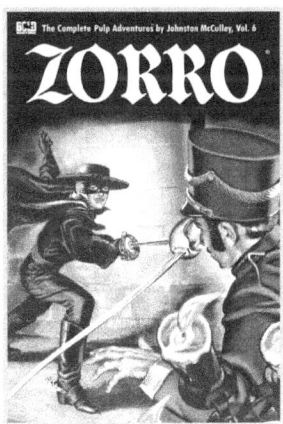

The Curse of Capistrano's original adventures —
collected for the first time in paperback and hardcover.

WWW.BOLDVENTUEPRESS.COM

The Curse of Capistrano's wildest adventure!

ZORRO ®

and the
LITTLE DEVIL

A novel of high-adventure by
New York Times best-selling author
Peter David

VENTURE
WWW.BOLDVENTUREPRESS.COM

ZORRO ®

SWORDPLAY AND ROMANCE

BOLD NEW ANTHOLOGY 15 SHORT STORIES!

WWW.BOLDVENTUREPRESS.COM

ZORRO SHANGHAIED!

ZORRO'S PACIFIC ODYSSEY
A Zorro adventure in three parts

Zorro and the Outward Journey
Zorro and the Forbidden Country
Zorro and the Deadly Homecoming
by Susan Kite

Zorro's newest and boldest adventure takes him from
Spanish California shores to forbidden China regions.
To survive, Diego de la Vega must navigate a strange
and hostile land where he is little more than a slave!

WWW.BOLDVENTUREPRESS.COM

www.ingramcontent.com/pod-product-compliance
Lightning Source LLC
Chambersburg PA
CBHW060423260626
47161CB00005B/1757